Leah swallowed hard. She toyed with the dinner napkin in her hand and finally looked up. She could barely stand looking Kay in the eye. "I'm sorry, Kay. I don't think you're right about this. I can't not compete for that scholarship."

Kay stared at Leah, too stunned to speak. "I can't believe you'd do this to Katrina!"

"Kay," Alex warned, "you mean well. But I think Leah has as much a right to compete for the Adams Scholarship as you have not to. It is up to each one of you."

Kay looked at Alex, then propped her chin on her hands. "I hadn't thought of it like that," she conceded. "Maybe Alex is right, Leah. But you have until tomorrow to think about it. You can still change your mind, you know." She paused, then brightened considerably. "Now I'm going to start calling around and get as many other girls as I can to drop out."

SECOND BEST
Satin Slippers #5

Elizabeth Bernard

FAWCETT GIRLS ONLY • NEW YORK

RLI: $\dfrac{\text{VL 7 \& up}}{\text{IL 8 \& up}}$

A Fawcett Girls Only Book
Published by Ballantine Books
Copyright © 1988 by Cloverdale Press, Inc.

Library of Congress Catalog Card Number: 88-91022

ISBN 0-449-13308-7

Manufactured in the United States of America

First Edition: June 1988

With special thanks to Baryshnikov Bodywear by Marika, K.D. Dids, and Freed of London.

for
Gina James

Chapter 1

"What do you suppose a Finola Darling will look like?" Leah Stephenson asked, craning her neck to get a better view of herself in the small mirror on the jewelry counter of the airport gift shop. It was a rainy late autumn day, and the wind blowing in from San Francisco Bay had wreaked havoc with her thick blond hair. Leah wrinkled her nose in distaste at her rosy-cheeked reflection, wishing, as she had so often since becoming a student at the San Francisco Ballet Academy, that she weren't the wholesome blue-eyed all-American type. She longed to look more exotic, in a dark-eyed, mysterious way that seemed more appropriate for a girl whose dream in life was to become a ballerina. She tucked the damp strands of hair back up into her dancer's bun and pushed the hairpins tight against her scalp, determined that the next time she went outside it would take a typhoon to work them out. When Leah turned away from the mirror, her eyes were sparkling with barely suppressed excitement.

Then she glanced at her friend Katrina, and her excitement faded fast. The painfully thin brown-eyed girl was biting her nails again and seemed on the verge of tears. Until a week ago, Leah had never seen Katrina Gray look anything but happy, and she definitely had never bitten her nails before. Katrina prided herself on her slender hands and always kept them well manicured.

Leah wanted to shake Katrina and tell her that whatever was wrong, it wasn't worth falling apart about. But although Katrina was a very popular girl, she was also a very private sort of person. Leah had met her back in September when they both began the school term as first-year students at the Academy. But in the few short months they had known each other, Katrina had seldom spoken of her home or her background. All Leah knew was that Katrina's parents ran some sort of ski resort in Vermont, and that she had an obnoxious little brother whose real name was Andrew but who called himself Android the Noid whom she adored and missed a whole lot.

Leah breathed a sigh of frustration and decided to try to cheer up Katrina. "This Finola creature," Leah commented with an airy wave of her hand, "should have sent a picture, of course. How are we ever supposed to recognize her when she gets off the plane?" Leah's voice rose to compete with a sudden blast of static from the public address system, which was followed by a garbled announcement—something about planes being delayed because of the thick fog blanketing the Bay area.

Katrina screwed up her thin face and waited for the announcer to finish talking. She glanced down at her hands and quickly jammed them into the pockets of her kelly-green rain jacket. "It'll be easy to spot her. She'll look like a dancer," Katrina pointed out. She paused, and a dreamy expression crossed her face. "I sort of picture her with dark hair, blue eyes, and very pale skin. The last Belinda Bishop novel I read had a heroine named Finola. She looked just like that." After a wistful sigh, Katrina went on. "Funny thing—that Finola loved to dance too." Katrina went back to biting her nails.

"Just what SFBA needs!" Leah exclaimed. "One of Belinda Bishop's helpless women. Madame Preston is going to love it. Finola will probably sight Pavlova's ghost waltzing across the Blue Studio in the middle of morning class, give a terrible shriek, and fling herself out the window before our very eyes." Leah flung one arm open wide, dramatically covered her eyes with the other arm, and pretended to sink in a dead faint against the display case. Behind her the earrings jangled on their rack, and the saleswoman cleared her throat in a way that made Leah straighten up fast and scurry to Katrina's side. Under her breath she concluded, "I don't think we need *that* variety of Finola around here at all."

Leah waited for Katrina's reaction. Generally any comment even remotely poking fun at Katrina's passion for gothic romances, and particularly for her favorite author, provoked a fiery outburst from the mild-mannered Vermont girl. Leah had baited her purposely just now, to get her out of the gloomies. But after a long moment's silence, she realized Katrina wasn't going to react at all. Leah glanced at her sideward, wondering if perhaps she had hurt her feelings. Katrina looked like one of those fuzzy photos on the cover of a romance novel, the tearjerker kind. Even Katrina's usually springy light brown curly hair had gone limp and flat.

Sometimes I have no tact! Leah thought, and gave a quick annoyed toss of her head. Only last night at the boardinghouse where she lived, she and her best friend, Alexandra Sorokin, had been talking about Katrina, how thin she was getting and how blue she'd been lately. No, Leah shouldn't have teased her just now at all. She was about to blurt out her apologies, when she realized that Katrina hadn't even been listening. She was lost in a display of birthday cards on a nearby revolving rack.

Katrina suddenly glanced up guiltily and put her hands back into her pockets. "Uh—what did you just say? Sorry, I wasn't really listening." Katrina sounded as if she'd just touched down after an expedition to outer space.

"Oh, it was nothing. I was just saying that—" Leah stopped for a second. "You're probably wrong about Finola. I bet she'll have red hair and freckles and small beady eyes."

"Could be," Katrina replied with a shrug. She looked back at the birthday card display and let out another sad sigh. Leah suddenly realized why Katrina was so down. It was Katrina's sixteenth birthday, and she thought not one of her friends at school had remembered.

Leah wanted to wish Katrina a happy birthday, but she couldn't. Pretending to forget Katrina's sweet sixteenth was a crucial part of the master plan. That way Katrina would be genuinely surprised by the party the girls were throwing that evening at Katrina's host family's house. Leah's job right now was to get Katrina's mind off her birthday.

Leah checked her Betty Boop watch. "Hmmm. Now that Finola's plane is going to be late, we've got time to eat."

"Eat?" Katrina repeated, picking up first one card, barely skimming it, then the next.

"I'm starved!" Leah moaned. "Come on," she urged, firmly taking a card from Katrina's hand and placing it back on the rack. "Let's go to the coffee shop."

She hurried Katrina out the door and down the hall toward the brightly lit fast-food joint. As the waitress cleared the booth, Leah wished she hadn't been the one chosen to carry out this particular phase of the surprise party plan.

Part one of the plan was easy and had gone off without a hitch, except for the fact it had left Katrina looking absolutely miserable. Not one student in Madame's class this morning had wished Katrina a happy birthday, though everyone there was coming to the party. No one complimented Katrina on her new leotard, just in case it turned out to be a birthday present from home. In Katrina's shoes, Leah would be feeling pretty rotten right now, too.

Part two had meant getting Katrina out of the house on an afternoon that seemed to be made for lounging around and listening to the rain. It was a much tougher assignment, but inspiration had finally struck Leah during lunch that day. Madame Preston, the director of the Ballet Academy, had appointed Leah as the one-girl welcoming committee for Finola Darling, who was this year's exchange student from the senior school of England's Royal Ballet. Since Finola would be living with the same host family as Katrina, it seemed only logical that Katrina go along to the airport to greet her new housemate. Still, it had taken plenty of prodding from Leah and an actual order from Katrina's house mom, Mrs. Wyndham, until Katrina finally removed herself from her cozy bedroom, where she was busy reading Belinda Bishop's current bestseller.

"Leah," Katrina said as they finally settled into a comfortable corner booth at the coffee shop. "I'm sorry I'm being such a jerk!" She unwrapped her scarf and folded it in a long neat rectangle. Before Katrina put it on the seat beside her, Leah reached out to finger it. It was the most beautiful scarf Leah had ever seen, all mustardy and gold with crismon threads running through it. Katrina's mother had woven it herself and Leah had loved it on first sight.

"How can you call yourself a jerk?" Leah remonstrated. She fiddled with the scarf a moment longer and wished there were some way to make Katrina feel better—without blowing the surprise party.

Katrina shrugged and took off her jacket. "It's pretty obvious, isn't it? I've been in a horrible mood all week. And everyone's been too polite to ask me why."

Leah winced at the note of real pain in Katrina's soft voice. Katrina wasn't sad only because of her birthday but because none of her friends had bothered to ask what was wrong when she was feeling so down. All at once Leah decided no surprise party was worth all this grief. She'd wish Katrina a happy birthday right then and swear her to secrecy. Katrina could simply act surprised when she walked into the house. And if she didn't—

well—then what was the big deal? Taking a deep breath, Leah began to explain, "Listen. The reason nobody wi—" but the arrival of the waitress cut her off.

Remembering the cake back at the Wyndhams, Leah limited herself to a diet soda and a fruit salad. Katrina ordered a mug of hot chocolate.

"Katrina—" Leah began the moment the waitress left for the kitchen.

"No, let me explain," Katrina interrupted. "I have to talk to somebody about it." Katrina ran her fingers through her curly hair and heaved a sigh. "It's well, it's not that I didn't trust you as a friend before today. Nothing like that," she assured Leah. "But it's so hard to talk about because—" Her voice broke a little. "It has to do with my dancing."

"Your *dancing*!" Leah exclaimed, relieved. "You're upset about your dancing?" She wriggled out of her yellow slicker and pulled off the hooded white sweatshirt she had worn over her soft blue and purple flannel skirt. When she looked up at Katrina again, Leah smiled. "You idiot! Everyone thought—" She stopped, not wanting to ruin the big surprise now. "Actually, I was worried that something else might be bothering you. How in the world could you possibly be upset about your dancing?" She leaned forward across the top of the table. "Only this morning Madame singled you out as having the lightest jump in the class. She said you look like one of those nineteenth-century Taglioni lithographs, and that someday you'll dance a wonderful *Giselle*."

Blushing, Katrina tried to interrupt. "But, Leah—"

"Don't but-Leah me!" Leah snorted and stripped

the wrapping off her straw with a sharp gesture. "Then Diana actually complimented you on your port de bras in rep class Wednesday—and there are very few people around the school *she* bothers to compliment!"

"Except Pamela Hunter," Katrina exclaimed. Glamorous, redheaded Pam was one of the least popular girls at SFBA, though for some reason the favorite of one or two faculty and company members, Diana Chang among them.

"And last but not at all least, you were mentioned in Robert Mooreland's review of the student gala in *Footnotes.* He said Kay had the makings of a brilliant choreographer, but you were the one dancer he singled out in the whole piece. Something about—" Leah put her forefinger to her lip and gazed up at the ceiling, trying to remember his exact words "—something about 'a delicate bud who will blossom into a flower of great radiance on the stage of American dance.' Something to that effect." Leah grinned at Katrina. Like the other students at school, Leah had teased Katrina when the review was posted on the callboard, and she had been calling her Rosebud ever since. But that didn't change the fact that everyone was delighted Katrina had been singled out as a promising dancer. She was well liked in the school and had recently been voted most popular student.

Katrina's mouth turned up in the barest hint of a smile, but it faded just as quickly. She looked even sadder than before. Leah couldn't believe it. What had she said wrong now?

Katrina tapped Leah's arm. "Don't worry, it's nothing you said." She sighed, then went on. "We're good friends, and I guess friends are supposed to provide shoulders to cry on, so here goes." Katrina leaned back in her seat and drew her feet up under her. "I've known for almost a week now, and I haven't breathed a word to anyone. I kept hoping it was all just a bad dream, that I'd wake up one morning and it would be gone. I figured if I didn't tell anyone, or talk about it out loud, then it couldn't be real." Katrina reached for her purse and fumbled with the drawstring on the handwoven bag. Her fingers hesitated a moment before she pulled out an envelope. It was a silly birthday card, like the ones on the gift-shop rack. How could a funny card make Katrina so blue if it wasn't because everyone had missed her birthday?

"I got this," Katrina explained slowly, "and now everything's different. How good my dancing is just doesn't matter—not anymore." She shook her head and her voice seemed to catch in her throat. She closed her eyes and held the card out to Leah. A sheet of yellow legal paper slipped out.

Leah looked at Katrina. "You want me to read this?"

Katrina sniffled, and Leah pretended she didn't see the tears welling up in Katrina's big brown eyes. Katrina nodded and picked up her cup of cocoa, though both of her hands were shaking.

Leah put down the card and unfolded the note. The blue ink had run in certain spots, as if someone had spilled water on it—or tears.

Dear Katrina:

Happy Sweet Sixteenth. It's strange having you so far away for such an important birthday. Andrew—sorry, I mean Android the Noid—has made me promise we will have a sweet sixteen party for you here in the front parlor of the inn at Christmas—with *pink* decorations. I said, "Of course we will."

I'm afraid the news about the inn itself is not so good. Tallying last summer's receipts left no doubt at all that the Grays are going to have to pull out of the innkeeping business. We're going to have to sell the inn to those nice people I told you about from Boston. The closing is next week, but we won't have to move out before next spring, so you'll have the same old house to come home to for Christmas. After that, we'll all have to do our bit to make things work. A retailer in Boston is interested in my hand-loomed products and your dad is going back to teaching biology. He landed a job for next year at Lakewood High, but of course it'll be rocky financially until we can pull ourselves out of debt. I already spoke to Miss Ruth and she'll take you for free at her Burlington studio—in exchange for your teaching some elementary ballet classes after school. So you won't have to give up dance entirely. And with a little luck—who knows, maybe a year or two down the road you can return to SFBA.

The small handwriting continued down the page, but Leah didn't bother to read further. She sat back heavily against the plastic upholstery of the booth and looked up at Katrina. "You can't come back here next semester?" Leah said in a shocked whisper. "You have to leave SFBA?"

Katrina nodded dismally and twisted her napkin into a tight little rope. "I don't even know where we're going to live. The inn and the farm were our home," she said, her voice shaky.

Leah barely stifled a gasp. "Where will you go?" she asked.

"Don't worry, we have tons of relatives," Katrina assured Leah. "It's not like we won't have a roof over our heads. We just can't live in someone else's place forever."

"No, no, of course not," Leah said, suddenly afraid she had embarrased Katrina. All at once little details she'd noticed about Katrina since September began to make sense: the beautiful handmade clothes, the way Katrina begged off when the kids headed for Chinatown, the fact that Katrina always ordered a small soda at Cocoa Nuts, a favorite SFBA hangout.

Katrina went on, obviously making a great effort to sound optimistic. "And Dad does have a new job. That's good."

"But," Leah said, "you can't just leave SFBA— and then come back. Why, two years from now it'll be—" Leah stopped, not sure she should continue.

"Say it," Katrina looked directly at Leah and attempted a smile. "Two years from now will be too late. Too late to become a ballerina. Two years from now I would be trying to get into a company—if I had stayed here and continued my training." Katrina's voice faded and she stared into space over Leah's shoulder. "I think," she finally said, "that if I—*when* I—leave here, I won't dance anymore. There's no real point to it, is there?" The disappointment in Katrina's voice was heartbreaking.

Leah shook her head and glared at her friend.

"Don't say that!" Leah exclaimed. "And you are *not* going to leave here, Katrina Gray."

Katrina returned her stare and tapped her right ear. "Didn't you hear me? I can't come back," she said. Her voice got louder and a couple of heads at nearby tables turned to look at them.

Leah didn't care who was staring. She continued, not bothering to lower her voice. "You are not leaving here. Not without a fight." She waited for the words to sink in, then repeated them slowly, her eyes glinting. "Not without a fight. You've worked too hard here not to fight tooth and nail to stay. You can't give up your whole future, all your dreams, just like that!" Leah snapped her fingers. "I won't let you—none of your friends will. And you know you'll have a lot of friends pulling for you on this one." Leah folded her arms across her chest and fixed her gaze on the other girl. "Besides," she said with great deliberation, "I don't think you'll let yourself give up just like that. You'd hate yourself if you didn't try your hardest to stay, Katrina."

Katrina dabbed at her eyes with the wide sleeve of her baggy sweater. "I appreciate what you're trying to say, Leah. But how can I fight it?" She gave a hopeless shrug and sank back into her seat.

"Go to Madame Preston. It's her school. She can make anything happen if she wants to."

"Go to Madame?" Katrina echoed. The Academy's director was a reserved, rather stern woman who had been a very famous ballerina with her own company many years before. Now she was even more renowned as a ballet teacher. Most of the SFBA students loved studying with her but tried to avoid dealing with her outside the confines of a dance studio.

"You have to go to her," Leah repeated.

Katrina squared her shoulders. "Leah, you happen to have a particularly good relationship with Madame. She likes you. She thinks of you as an exceptionally talented student. If you were in my shoes, maybe she would pull all the strings she could to find a way to keep you at school. But Madame barely knows my name. She's always calling me Katherine! And I've never said three words to her outside of class. How can I ask her for money? Besides, the registrar, Mrs. Dodsworth, is in charge of money—not Madame."

Leah didn't answer right away. Katrina had made a good point, and Leah could certainly understand her reluctance to approach the formidable Madame Preston. She was tempted to confide in Katrina and tell her the truth about her own relationship with Madame: It wasn't as cozy as Katrina seemed to think. Only a few weeks after the semester began, Leah had felt the full fury of the director's wrath when she had gotten mixed up in James Cummings's scheme to hide the fact he was injured from the instructors at SFBA. As a result, James had had a terrible accident at a dance demonstration at a local high school. Madame Preston had not been very understanding when Leah had told her side of the story. In fact, she had been downright furious. Leah's punishment had been over for weeks now, but ever since her run-in with the school director, Leah had tried to avoid crossing her path. She couldn't fault Katrina for being reluctant to approach Madame.

"I know Madame can be difficult," Leah said.

"But she's no fool. She knows how tough it is for parents to pay tuition here. And you have no choice, Katrina. You *have* to ask her for help. Between her and Mrs. Dodsworth they'll be able to come up with something. They'll have to," Leah concluded with great conviction.

Katrina regarded Leah in silence. Slowly, her brown eyes lit up. "You're right. My future does depend on this, and I can't just give up without a fight. I'll talk to her on Monday, right after class." Katrina sighed loudly. "But I can't afford to get my hopes up. I couldn't bear to be so disappointed again." Katrina lowered her eyes to the table. "I've begun to accept the fact that I have to go home. There can't be that much scholarship money left by this time of the year. And in spite of what you say, I am not one of our class's star students."

Before Leah could argue the point, a slim, well-built man with a dark mustache and sparkling brown eyes hurried up to the booth. Raul Zamora, an actor and director of San Francisco's experimental Teatro Hispánico, taught fencing and drama at the SFBA in exchange for this theater troupe getting to study dance at the Academy. He also helped out around the school, taking care of odds and ends, and he had driven the Academy van to the airport to pick up Finola.

"There you are," he said, a bit breathless. "I've been scouring the place for you two." His eyes rested a moment on Katrina's face. She didn't look as gloomy now, and behind Katrina's back Raul gave Leah an approving wink. "Finola's flight has finally landed. I think I just spotted some British Airways passengers coming through customs."

"Oh!" Katrina cried, grabbing her scarf. "She'll think we forgot all about her! Imagine arriving in a strange country and having no one there to meet you."

"Finola won't have time to worry if we hurry," Raul said.

Leah picked up the check before Katrina could protest and tossed some change on the table for a tip. Then she grabbed her things, paid the cashier, and hurried out of the coffee shop after Katrina and Raul.

By the time she caught up to them, they were already standing underneath the International Arrivals sign. They were scrutinizing the steady stream of passengers as they emerged from several sets of glass-paned double doors, but it was Leah who spotted the exchange student first.

She cupped her hands over her mouth and called out, "Finola Darling!" Her voice was swallowed in the noise of the crowd. "There," she said to Katrina, grabbing her hand. "She's over there." With her other hand Leah waved wildly in the direction of a slender girl with the most beautiful complexion and the biggest eyes Leah had ever seen. Her hair was dark and piled on top of her head in a bun that looked very much like Leah's. "See. That's got to be her," Leah cried excitedly. She directed Katrina's gaze to a group of people on the left of a nearby column. "In the I Love to Dance T-shirt."

"I was right!" Katrina clapped her hands together and bounced up and down a little on her toes. "Finola, over here!" she yelled at the top of her lungs.

The tall, thin girl looked blankly in their direction. All at once she did a silly little pirouette, with one arm above her head, then gave them a questioning look. Leah and Katrina nodded vigorously, and Raul waved.

Finola smiled. Even from this distance Leah could see a friendly dimple on one of her cheeks. "I was right," Katrina said smugly to Leah. "You owe me ten of something—I don't remember exactly what we bet." She craned her neck to get a better look at Finola. "She *does* look like a Belinda Bishop heroine!" she declared with a contented smile.

Chapter 2

The girls climbed into the royal blue San Francisco Ballet Academy van with the logo of two dancers painted on the doors, and Katrina was still smiling. She whispered to Leah over the stiff wind that whistled across the airport loading area, "But Finola is not like a Belinda Bishop heroine at all!"

Leah nodded wholeheartedly and quickly checked out Finola for the umpteenth time since she had arrived. The English girl was taller than Leah by a couple of inches, and was anything but just another pretty ballet student: Finola was very beautiful and she looked older than sixteen. While Raul tossed Finola's suitcase and duffel bags into the cargo area of the van, she leaned against the open back doors, talking in a high birdlike voice that somehow seemed at odds with her dramatic appearance. In spite of her faded jeans and her oversize T-shirt, now only partly visible beneath her long black baggy drawstring jacket, Finola certainly looked the part of a leading lady in a gothic romance. Her black hair contrasted with her pale complexion beautifully, and her gray eyes were fringed with long black lashes.

At the same time, mysterious and romantic were words that didn't seem to suit Finola at all. When she smiled, her face lit up brightly, and her laugh was so warm and heartfelt that it cheered up even Katrina. Leah decided right there and then that they were destined to be great friends.

Until Leah had come to SFBA, she had always trusted her instincts about people. But after a week at the school she had learned never to make snap judgments again. She had been horribly wrong about Alexandra Sorokin, whom she had practically hated at first sight, and who was now one of her best friends. She had been equally wrong about Pamela Hunter, who had been very sweet when Leah had first met her, but who had quickly proven herself to be anything but a friend. There was something about Finola that made Leah like her right from the start, despite her warnings to herself. Leah was sure SFBA was going to be a lot more fun while this particular exchange student was around.

"So don't you think this T-shirt was a perfectly *smashing* idea!" Finola held her shirt out and beamed at it. She hopped into the van and clambered over the seats. She sat down next to Leah.

"It was helpful!" Leah laughed and returned the other girl's friendly smile.

Raul pulled out onto the highway and Finola pressed her nose against the window, surveying the neighborhood as they drove by.

"Are my digs far from here?" Finola asked. She put her hand over her mouth and yawned.

Katrina poked her head over the front seat. "No. It's a short trip, unless there's traffic." With a shy smile she added, "We're going to be housemates at the Wyndhams!"

Leah was glad that Katrina and Finola would be in the same house. Finola's enthusiasm and infectious smile might be just what Katrina needed to lift her spirits and inspire her to fight to stay at the Academy.

Finola leaned back and propped her ankles up behind Katrina's seat. "That's great, Katrina," she said with a comfortable sigh. "I was afraid I'd get here and not know a soul and have to walk into class the first time all by myself." She smiled first at Katrina and then at Leah. "So double thanks for coming to get me."

Raul caught Finola's eyes in the rearview mirror. "Madame Preston wouldn't have it any other way. She wants her students to feel right at home."

"I like that!" Finola commented. "It was hard leaving London and all my friends. I've been in school with some of them since I was eleven years old."

"Do you board at the school?" Leah asked.

"I did back then. Now that I'm in the upper school, I don't. I live with my aunt Maude and uncle George not far from Baron's Court, where the school is. It's very nice and convenient." Finola winked at Raul's back, then poked Leah playfully in the ribs. "But I say, it'll be jolly good fun not living with family," she whispered to Leah. "I'll miss my friends at school and my aunt and uncle, but I definitely will not miss my five little cousins!"

Raul exited from the highway and turned down the side street that led to the school.

Katrina leaned forward in her seat and peered through the windshield at the foggy street. "Hey," she objected, "we're going the wrong way."

"No, we're not," Raul replied. "We're going up to the Academy first. I thought Finola might like to see the scene of the crime right away." His face creased into a pleasant smile.

Finola frowned at his reflection in the mirror. "Won't I have plenty of time to see it tomorrow? I've got so much unpacking to do and I'm rather tired. I was thinking of a two-hour bath myself." She looked down the length of her outstretched legs and wriggled her toes. She had kicked off her loafers, and a pair of socks painted with yellow and red suns and clouds decorated her strongly arched feet. "It'll take precisely that long to get the wrinkles out of my muscles. I feel like I've been permanently pressed into a sitting position."

"Yeah, Raul. Let's just head home," Katrina urged. She checked the watch that hung loosely on her tiny wrist. "Finola's tired and so am I. And I promised Mrs. Wyndham we'd be back in time for dinner."

Raul looked helplessly at Leah in the mirror. When they had discussed this part of the surprise party plan, neither of them had expected so much resistance from Katrina.

Leah took her cue. "No," Leah said, "Raul's right. We won't make it a long tour, but Finola"— Leah drew her legs up under her and kneeled on the seat facing the English girl—"you're going to absolutely love the place. It's so much better than those silly pictures in the catalog. The grounds and the house itself are great, not to mention the classrooms. Wait until you see the studios! When I first saw the Academy, I thought I was dreaming." Leah raced on with her description, not giving the other girls a chance to object. The surprise part of Katrina's party depended on them

not showing up at the Wyndhams until six-thirty
P.M. They still had forty-five minutes to waste.

"Well, it's no big deal to me either way." Finola
spoke up after a long series fo yawns. "But just
don't make it the *grand* tour, or you might have
to carry me into my new home."

Raul slicked back his closely cropped hair and
chuckled. "Like a regular Sleeping Beauty!" He
turned into the gravel driveway leading to the
school's side entrance. From this angle, the stately
Victorian mansion was almost completely hidden
behind a wall of tall trees whose tops vanished in
the mist.

Before he had even turned off the motor, Leah
jumped out. "Come on, Finola!" Leah practically
pulled Finola out of the van. "The view of the
school itself isn't great from this end, but you can
see that later. Look," she cried, pointing to the
lights of the Golden Gate Bridge just visible beyond
the confines of the school property. "Isn't it wonderful?" she oozed.

Finola cocked her head and looked impressed.
"So that's San Francisco Bay," she said. She started
walking confidently across the dark lawn to get a
better glimpse of the foggy twilight vista, her loafers
making loud squishy noises in the soggy grass.

Leah followed at her heels and cleared her
throat. Then she whispered, "Hey—sorry to bring
you here now. I know you're tired but—"

"But you wanted me to see the school," Finola
said loudly.

"Not exactly." Leah glanced back toward the
main building of the school. Katrina was making
no move to follow them, so she spoke in a more
normal tone. "It's Katrina's sixteenth birthday today and we're throwing a party—"

"I get it!" Finola whooped with glee. *"A surprise party!!!!!"* Quickly she clapped her hand over her mouth. "I blew it, didn't I?" she wailed. "Me and my big mouth. And I don't have a present for her," she added, distressed. "That's an awkward bit, isn't it? Seeing she's my flatmate and all!"

"Katrina would never expect a gift from you," Leah hastened to explain. "And you didn't ruin it." Not yet, she said to herself, a bit nervous about Finola's outburst. "She didn't hear you, anyway." Finola and Leah looked back together toward the mist-shrouded building. The twilight had deepened, and between the dark and the fog, Raul and Katrina looked like blurry shadows. "I had to explain our plan to you," Leah went on in a rush. "We have to kill time here, so I want you to act very interested in *everything.*"

Finola straightened up and winked at Leah. "No problem. I'll ask about the wallpaper, the light fixtures, the finish on the studio floors, and how old the staircase is. I usually talk so much she'll never suspect a thing," she assured Leah.

"Perfect!" Leah sighed with relief. "But don't be too obvious about it," she warned.

"Don't worry, I'm a natural at this," Finola said. "But you know, she's probably expecting some kind of party. I am always convinced someone is going to throw me a surprise party on my birthday. But all my birthday parties end up being planned, and no one's surprised me yet. Of course, maybe that's because I expect one all the time." Leah wasn't sure she followed Finola's logic, but she was glad to have her in on the scheme.

As they strolled back to the main building, Finola asked, "Do you think she knows about the party?"

"No, she has no idea!" Leah said, confident. She's too upset about—" Leah stopped herself. She wasn't about to divulge Katrina's personal problems to a girl she'd just met an hour ago.

"*Shhhh,*" Finola whispered. A moment later Katrina marched up, her hand planted on her hips and her lips drawn in a tight thin line.

"I thought this was supposed to be a quick tour of the school," Katrina said.

"It will be, it will be," Leah assured her.

"But not so quick that I don't get a chance to get the—the feel of it, the *ambiance,*" Finola added, faking a heavy French accent. She hooked one hand through Raul's arm and one through Katrina's and led them to the door. Just as she stepped over the threshold she turned back and smiled at Leah.

Leah quickly put her finger to her lips and held her breath.

"Tell me how long the school's been here," Finola said to Raul. "Wasn't there some kind of historic earthquake around here? Was this building here then?"

Just inside the door Raul pulled out his light key and switched on the overheads for the foyer and downstairs halls.

Finola let out a delighted little cry. "It's an old mansion!" she exclaimed. She stood perfectly still, gaping wide-eyed at the high ceiling. Her gaze traveled to the sparkly crystal chandelier and the stained glass window above the impressive oak front door. She touched the delicately flowered wallpaper above the highly polished wainscoting. "Now I see why you fell in love with this place at first sight," she said to Leah.

"It's a Victorian landmark now," Raul commented. "Part of the building survived the big quake. The rest was rebuilt by the millionaire who owned it at that time." He turned on the other lights and motioned toward the grand staircase leading to the floors above. "Why don't you girls show Finola the upstairs while I check on something in the basement? With all this rain, there could be flooding."

Leah was barely able to keep a straight face when Raul said that. The two of them had picked up a dark chocolate cake specially ordered from Cocoa Nuts and hidden it in the cafeteria refrigerator before leaving for the airport. Raul was probably going to stow it in the van while the girls explored the building.

Suddenly Katrina started to follow Raul, and Leah rushed to block her way. "There's nothing much to see in the basement," she said. Katrina gave her a strange look and continued toward the back stairs. Leah positioned herself on the top step and tried to think fast. She just had to keep Katrina away from the basement and the cake. "Really, Katrina," Leah repeated a little louder. "Finola couldn't care less about the basement."

"That's true. I don't really fancy basements. They're dark and damp and creepy." Turning to Leah, she asked, "And didn't Raul say something about a flood!" She gave a convincing little shiver. "And to think I came to California for the sunshine!"

"See, Katrina. Finola really doesn't want to go downstairs. I don't blame her. After all, it's so boring down there," Leah said, leaning strategically against the wall and blocking the way. Katrina would have to do a grand jeté over her to get down those stairs.

Katrina stared at Leah as if she had lost her

mind. "Boring?" She rolled her eyes and made a helpless gesture with her hands. "Very boring, the pits, really," she said, her voice full of sarcasm. "Just the dance tape library—which is almost as good as the one they have at Lincoln Center in New York City. Our costume and sewing room. Half the academic classrooms. And best of all, the lunchroom." Katrina had obviously decided to appeal directly to Finola and ignore Leah completely. "Wait until you meet Mr. Mom—I mean, Mr. Momous. Of course he won't be here today because it's Saturday, but he runs the lunch program and he can really cook." Katrina rubbed her stomach and added wistfully. "I sure could go for one of his lunches. But at least we have a vending machine now. Come on, I'll show you. It's got fruit and juice and other healthy stuff, in case you're on a diet." She tried to push past Leah.

"Later!" Leah commanded in a shrill little yelp. She grabbed the elbow of Katrina's sweater and tugged her toward the front door, hoping that whatever she was going to say next wouldn't sound ridiculous. "I think Finola is far more interested in where she gets to dance and what the studios look like than where we eat lunch or the new vending machine. And I'm sure she couldn't care less about where we study history."

"Absolutely," Finola said promptly. "I'm not at all hungry!" Finola declared. Just then her stomach gave a loud grumble and Leah tried not to giggle.

Katrina smiled at Finola. "You may not be hungry, but your stomach sure is."

"Ah-uh-oh-well, of course. You see, I just dropped a half stone—" Seeing the blank expression on Leah and Katrina's faces, Finola translated quickly,

"That's about seven pounds. And I need to lose some more. I don't think I want to make the acquaintance of a vending machine just yet."

"You're on a diet!" Leah and Katrina both exclaimed, looking with disbelief in their eyes at the slender girl.

"Of course, that's how you stay so thin," Leah improvised quickly, realizing her mistake. "We don't want to tempt poor Finola off her diet, do we?" she asked Katrina. "That wouldn't be very nice of us on her first day here," she pointed out.

"Okay, we'll save the cafeteria until tomorrow," Katrina gave in with a sigh. She cast one last longing glance toward the back stairs and plopped herself on the bottom step of the sweeping staircase that led to the second floor.

Leah decided to go on with Finola's tour. "I wanted you to get the exact feel of what it will be like to walk in here for class Monday morning," she said.

"Walking in here first thing in the morning feels awful, Leah," Katrina observed. "Stop grinning and admit it. You've just walked about half a mile to get here, your eyes closed the whole way. And if you don't eat breakfast, like me, your stomach is complaining every step of the way until you're about halfway through your pliés!"

Finola chuckled. "Sounds just like home." Spotting Leah's face, Finola wiped the smile off her own and looked sheepish.

Leah decided to ignore Katrina's objections and continue. "First thing you should do, Madame always says, is check the call-board. When you're in a professional company, that's very important, and it's best to get in the habit here." She took a few comical waddling steps, greatly exaggerating her turnout, and peered at the bulletin board that hung on the wall beside the front stairs. Finola followed behind Leah, aping her every move.

Katrina giggled.

"We've got one of these too," Finola said. "Usually it's got grades and audition results and all sorts of notices on it about rehearsals, change of classrooms, and, of course, lots of lost-and-founds: toe shoes, ribbons, and socks."

"Toe shoe notices go downstairs, on the little corkboard near the cafeteria," Katrina said, stressing the last word.

Finola stared at the neatly typed lists of names and index cards posted on the board. She stretched her long arms over her head as if she were working out a kink in her back. Throwing her weight onto one hip, she read aloud:

Four senior boys needed for performances with Oakland experimental dance troupe. Must be at least five foot eight inches tall with some gymnastic and partnering experience. Tap-dance training helpful. Limited engagement at local theater area. Contact Melissa Peters for additional audition information. 555-1249, after 12 noon.

"So students here can actually dance with professional companies?" Finola sounded surprised.

"With permission, and not very often," Leah replied.

Finola turned her attention back to the board. "Hey, what's this?"

Leah stepped to her side and peered over Finola's shoulder as she read aloud from the typewritten sheet:

Competition for the Louise Adams Scholarship
will be held this Wednesday. The scholarship will pay full tuition and board for two
years, and the winner will perform the lead
in this year's student production of *Giselle* in
the Academy auditorium on the Louise Adams Scholarship evening next month.

"What!" Both Leah and Katrina exclaimed in
the same breath. Leah whirled around and came
face-to-face with Katrina. The brown-haired girl
had sprung to her feet.

"A scholarship? Are you sure?" Katrina asked.
"Who's eligible?" She pushed Leah and Finola
aside and read on, her voice trembling. "The competition is open to all first- and second-year girls
currently attending the San Francisco Ballet Academy on a full-time basis, and who are American
citizens."

"What a bummer!" Finola sighed. "The tuition
part doesn't matter, since the exchange program
makes this year free for me, but I sure would love
to dance *Giselle.*" Finola hummed a few bars of
the score and began to dance her way down the
hall, pretending to have her fingers on a partner's
arm. She smiled at her imaginary danseur and
coyly pretended she was pulling the petals off a
daisy. "He loves me," she said in a sweet voice,
"he loves me not!"

Leah watched Finola critically and couldn't quite
believe what she was seeing. Finola hadn't danced
more than a couple of steps, wearing bulky street
clothes, but she looked exactly the way the delicate peasant girl, Giselle, should look: light, frail,
buoyant, and very naive. In fact, she looked as if
she had been performing the part for years.

"Oh, Leah!" Katrina cried, grabbing Leah's hands and spinning her around and around in a circle. She stopped suddenly and Leah felt a little dizzy. Katrina looked back at the notice, her smile ecstatic. "Is this fate or what? I just can't believe the timing!" She drew a sharp breath and pressed her hands to her chest. "You were right. Something *did* turn up. I feel like the goddess of dance has reached down from the sky and rescued me!"

"Saved you from having that talk with Madame, that's for sure." Leah grinned broadly, relieved Katrina wouldn't have to go through that ordeal.

Instantly Finola stopped humming and she walked back to the other girls. Looking at Katrina, she asked in a concerned voice, "Was something wrong?"

Katrina dropped her gaze and a slow blush crept up her neck and face. "No point in hiding the truth anymore. Besides, we're going to be housemates." Katrina looked up and gave Finola a weak smile. "My family's having some money problems," she confessed. "If this scholarship opportunity hadn't come along, I'd definitely be leaving at the end of this semester."

Finola whistled softly under her breath. She hooked her thumbs in the back pockets of her jeans and regarded Katrina a moment before speaking. "That's terrible. Really, it is," she said, her voice soft and sympathetic. "But if you win, love, your troubles will be over!" Finola smiled at Katrina, full of optimism.

Katrina stared back at Finola, her eyes widening. Slowly she said, "Of course. How could I be so dumb?" She folded her arms across her chest. "I have to *win*, don't I? It's a competition, not a gift from some goddess of dance." She bit her lower lip and leaned back against the bulletin board, her soft frizzy hair fanning out across the bottom of the notice. "I don't even want to think of who'll be competing."

"Then don't," Leah advised quickly. "Don't you dare think of anyone else. Think of yourself, Katrina, and do your best. That's what Madame said during the entrance auditions, don't you remember?"

Katrina looked blank. Obviously she couldn't care less about what Madame said. She was biting her nails again and staring dully at the opposite wall.

Leah put her hands on Katrina's shoulders and gave her a little shake, suddenly conscious of how thin and fragile Katrina was. "Madame said the only real competition we ever have is ourselves. I had to keep thinking that when I danced my solo for the audition. Pam stole it from me, remember?" Katrina nodded. "I had to tell myself that it didn't matter how well she danced it, or how strong she is, or how brilliant her technique happens to be. I kept telling myself over and over that the person I had to beat was myself, not Pam. If I had let myself think for one second how the odds were stacked against me, I would never have danced well. Just dance your best, Katrina."

"That's easy for you to say!" Katrina snapped. She wriggled free of Leah's grasp. "You're the best dancer in the whole class. You—won the Golden Gate Award, and they almost never give that to a new girl. It's easy for you to say just do your best."

During Katrina's outburst, Leah was conscious of Finola standing beside her, sizing her up, trying to figure out if Katrina had exaggerated Leah's abilities. Leah hated that feeling of looking at other girls as if they were just competition, and not friends or even people at all. Of course she had just done more or less the same thing to Finola a moment ago, trying to figure out how good she really was, and where she would fall in the scheme of things as far as school politics were concerned, once Madame Preston saw her dance in class.

Leah forced herself to ignore Finola, though, and focus on Katrina's worry. "There's no best dancer in this school. A hundred or so girls competed to get in, and you, Katrina Gray, were one of the fifteen chosen. So stop feeling sorry for yourself."

Katrina stared at Leah in shock. "If you want to give up and decide you haven't got a chance for that scholarship," Leah went on, "then give up right now. It's your life and your career that's on the line." Leah shrugged. She walked over to the main staircase and beckoned Finola to follow her. Then she added, "But I know if Madame had said to me—even once—that *I* was born to dance *Giselle,* wild horses couldn't keep me from trying out for the part and the Adams scholarship as well."

Katrina was still staring aghast at Leah. Finola marched over to Leah's side and nodded in agreement. She looked over her shoulder at Katrina, waiting for her to join them for the rest of the tour. "Katrina does look like Giselle!" She tugged Leah's sleeve in excitement. "Don't you see it? I've been in a few competitions like this back home, and the judges always give the role to the student who is most suited to it—the one who looks the part."

"They do?" Katrina sounded skeptical.

Finola just nodded. "And I bet when you show up at the competition, they are going to take one look at you and practically give you the role without your even dancing a step."

"She's right," Leah added. "You're bound to get it, Katrina. And you don't just *look* right either. No one in class dances Giselle's solos like you! You do the best hops on pointe of anyone."

Katrina regarded Leah with some suspicion. She slowly twined a strand of her hair around her finger, then untwined it. "You're not just saying that?"

Leah shook her head solemnly.

"Look, we can't guarantee you'll get it, no one can," Finola cautioned. "But you have a better chance than most of the other girls, I bet." Finola suddenly clapped her hands together sharply. "And you know what? Since I can't compete, I'll help you, Katrina. I coached a student in my old school for *Fille Mal Gardée,* and she got the role."

Katrina began to smile. "That would be great! Thanks." Her grin widened as she talked. "I'm going to try to forget about how good everyone else is, and I'm going to try to win."

Leah gave Katrina a meancing look and tapped her foot sharply against the polished parquet floor.

Katrina's grin softened to a sheepish smile. "Okay, Leah, I get the point. I *am* going to win." Turning to Finola, she said, "And I'll accept help from you or anyone else who has the time. I'll need it." She bit her lip and shyly regarded her feet. When she looked up again, her brown eyes were glinting wickedly. "Let me promise you one thing, Leah Stephenson, I'm going to be around SFBA long enough for you to get sick of me and wish you hadn't given me this little pep talk!"

"Pep talk?" Leah feigned ignorance. She looked at Finola, her face all innocence.

Finola played dumb, too. She shrugged her expressive shoulders. "What pep talk?"

"Beats me," Leah concluded, and nimbly swerved out of Katrina's reach as Katrina threatened to hit her with her tiny fist. Leah bounded up the steps and yelled back over her shoulder at the girls clattering after her, "Observe carefully, Ms. Darling! SFBA's special fifty-stair dash to Madame's morning class!"

Chapter 3

"Surprise!!!!" The chorus of voices was so loud that Katrina reeled back slightly through the open front door and landed smack against Leah's chest. Leah grunted, then grabbed Katrina's shoulders and pushed her right back across the threshold into the spacious foyer of the Wyndhams' home.

"For me?" Katrina gasped. "All this?" Her eyes were bright with tears, and an incredulous smile spread across her face. She remained speechless for a moment, just staring at the crowd: It seemed the whole school had turned up, not just first-year ballet students. Some faculty members were there, and so was Mr. Mom, the cook, who had made it his personal mission to fatten up delicate Katrina. Katrina gazed in awe at the green, pink, and white crepe streamers, the Happy Birthday bannner strung across the living room entrance, the bouquet of bright balloons that hovered near the ceiling just above a table laden with trays of sandwiches, cold cuts, cookies, bowls of fruit, and potato chips, and a huge pink, green, and white frosted cake.

Leah followed Katrina's glance to the cake and marveled. How in the world had Raul gotten it here? She looked back over her shoulder to ask him. He had brought up the rear of the small procession from the van through the pouring rain to the Wyndhams' doorstep. He stood behind Finola, shaking out his big striped umbrella and grinning. Leah wanted to hug him, but she didn't get a chance. All at once the whole crowd pressed forward into the foyer to personally wish Katrina a happy birthday.

Kay Larkin's short curly hair bobbed as she helped Katrina take off her jacket. "So you're really surprised? You aren't just faking it?" Kay asked.

"Faking it!" Katrina squeezed Kay's arm hard. "If I even suspected a party, I'd never have left the house dressed like this." She examined her old baggy sweater and faded jeans and patted her mop of wet curls. "Why, I look just awful!" she wailed, craning her neck to get a glimpse of herself in the small oval wall mirror.

"You look beautiful!" Alexandra Sorokin said, and then turned to Leah, smiling, a soft glow in her almond-shaped dark eyes. "Leah, I just knew you were the right person to pull off this party."

Leah basked in the compliment, glad she hadn't let her friends down. She'd come terribly close to blowing the whole thing back at the airport. Remembering the airport made Leah think of Finola. She hooked her own rain slicker on one of the curved oak arms of the antique coatrack, and looked for the British girl. Finola was leaning against the doorframe, peacefully regarding the commotion and trying to stifle a yawn.

"Alex," Leah shouted above the din of the crowd.

"This is Finola Darling, the new girl from the Royal Ballet School in London." Finola held out her hand and Alex shook it warmly. Leah noted that Alex and Finola were exactly the same height.

"I am Alexandra Sorokin."

Finola recognized the name instantly. "Your parents—don't tell me—they're Olga and Dimitri Sorokin?" Her gray eyes darkened with appreciation as Alex nodded. "I didn't realize they had a daughter. Or rather," she added, turning to Leah, "that she'd be a student here, in the States."

"I've lived in America since I was about eleven," Alex informed her. "My parents defected from the Kirov while I was an exchange student in Canada. That is why I was able to join them here. But that is old news. The big news is that it is Katrina's sixteenth birthday. I hope Leah warned you about this." Alex hooked her arm through Finola's and guided her through the crowd into the living room.

"Yes, she told me about the party when we were at the school."

Finola's high-pitched voice carried easily over the general din, and Katrina spun around.

"Leah Stephenson," she scolded. "You knew all about this. You knew!" Katrina accused her, a silly grin spreading right from one ear to the other. "And I fell for it. I didn't suspect a thing. First you dragged me to the airport with you—" Katrina's hand flew to her mouth and she eyed Finola ruefully. "I'm glad you did, really I am," she added apologetically. "And then to think I actually fell for that silly tour of the Academy in the pouring rain. I didn't even remember it was my birthday!" she concluded, amazed.

Several voices exclaimed that was impossible, but Leah bit her lower lip. Katrina had been far too preoccupied with thoughts of her future as a dancer to think about birthdays.

"I didn't think it was a silly tour at all," Finola said. She edged her way into the living room and grabbed a sandwich. "I think it was wonderful. And just think, Katrina, if we hadn't gone there, you wouldn't have found out about the Adams scholarship and the chance to dance *Giselle.*"

"*Giselle?*" Alex practically spilled the cup of fruit punch she held in her hand. "The notice said *Giselle*?"

Katrina, Leah, and Finola nodded. Alex seemed about to say more, but just then Clarissa Wyndham, Katrina's house mother, walked up. She hugged Katrina and handed her a tiny, beautifully wrapped package. She had a fur coat over one arm, and her purse in her hand. Obviously, she and her husband had decided to clear out and give the party the run of the house. There were more than enough other chaperons present.

"You must be Finola Darling!" Mrs. Wyndham said with a gracious smile. "Welcome. We're glad to have you here for the rest of the year, and I know Katrina will be ecstatic to finally have someone her own age around to liven up this big old house." She said that with a smile and paused to tousle Katrina's damp curls. Katrina looked so happy at that moment, Leah ached to think that without a bit of luck she might have to leave all of this behind. Turning again to Finola, Mrs. Wyndham went on. "Your room is just at the top of the stairs to the left of the bathroom. Perhaps you can prevail on some of the boys to help Raul with your luggage." As she started out the door, the house mother called back over her shoulder, "We'll have lots of time to get acquainted tomorrow. Katrina can show you where everything is in the meantime. Enjoy yourself tonight!"

As Mrs. Wyndham ducked under her husband's umbrella and headed out into the night, Finola declared, "I like her, and it's going to be great living here. It's so homey!" She gave a comfortable sort of shrug and looked down the bookcase-lined hall toward the open doors of the spacious kitchen.

"I know you will!" Leah agreed. "Mrs. Wyndham's really nice and this is the wildest old house. Ask Katrina to show you the trunks full of old dance and opera costumes in the attic sometime. You lucked out—two girls just moved because they got jobs in southern California with a regional company." Leah popped a couple of peanuts into her mouth and slowly proceeded into the living room as she continued to fill Finola in on her new hostess's background. "Clarissa Wyndham knows more about dance than almost anyone around here, except Madame and the librarian, of course. She used to study when she was a young girl, but when she was thirteen or so, she just got too big."

Finola grimaced. Reaching puberty and turning out to have the wrong body type for ballet was the kind of nightmare every girl who had ever studied ballet seriously had had. There wasn't a student at SFBA who hadn't been scared out of her wits to become a teenager, afraid she'd wake up one morning inches too tall, or a little too curvy, or just the wrong shape for a classical ballerina.

As they entered the living room, Alex walked up. She took Finola's hand and pulled her toward a group of kids chatting animatedly. "So you can meet more of the gang," Alex explained, and Finola gave Leah a helpless little wave as she was dragged off.

Leah smiled back in an absent sort of way. She leaned against the side of the grand piano and slowly opened a diet soda, not really paying attention to what she was doing. She kept thinking of Mrs. Wyndham, and Katrina, and the problem of Katrina's parents running out of money in another couple of months. All of a sudden Leah gasped aloud and almost choked on her soda. Why hadn't she and Katrina thought of it first thing? Leah was positive that Mrs. Wyndham could find a way for Katrina to stay at the Academy. Leah looked around for Katrina; she wanted to tell her right away, to take some of the awful pressure off winning the scholarship competition.

Just then Raul clapped his hands together to get everyone's attention. Leah looked over toward the table where the candles on the cake had been lit: sixteen of them around the edges, and right in the center, planted squarely on the ribbons of frosting that made the shape of a pair of tiny pink toe shoes, was the seventeenth candle, the one for good luck. Katrina was standing in front of the cake, looking very embarrassed. From across the room Kenny Rotolo started the chorus of "Happy Birthday." Katrina sank back against the tablecloth and looked as if she wanted the floor to open up and swallow her. It was definitely not Katrina Gray's style to be the center of attention. She was blissfully happy, but even from her vantage point Leah could see Katrina was on the brink of tears.

Leah elbowed her way closer to Katrina so that when the song was over she could hug her and tell her things were going to work out all right. Meanwhile, she began singing "Happy Birthday," even though her voice was high and tinny and flat as a pancake. She sang with all her might, wanting to wish Katrina the best of luck. Another voice chimed in, one Leah didn't recognize. Leah and several other kids turned in the direction of the lovely birdlike voice. It was Finola.

From over Leah's shoulder, Linda Howe whispered, "If she can dance half as well as she can sing, the competition around this place is going to be stiffer than ever!"

Leah nodded. She had had the exact same thought. Then all at once everyone was clapping and Katrina bent over the cake to blow the candles out. Leah held her breath and crossed her fingers, knowing exactly what Katrina's wish would be. Katrina managed to blow out sixteen candles, but the center one, the one for good luck, refused to go out.

"Try again!" Michael Litvak yelled.

"But it won't count!" Katrina said, her voice quavering.

"Yes, it will!" Finola spoke up and marched right up to the table. "In England we say if you get it the second time round, you'll get twice the luck!" She caught Leah's eye as she said that, and Leah had a feeling Finola had just made that up so that Katrina wouldn't get discouraged about the scholarship.

Katrina took a deep breath and blew as hard as she could. The candle finally went out. Everyone cheered, then Michael and Kenny began chanting, "Speech! Speech!" Patrick Hogan, one of the teachers at SFBA, lifted Katrina on top of a chair.

"Speech?" Katrina squeaked. She looked around

the room helplessly, from Leah to Linda, from Kay to Alex.

"I don't know how to thank you all for this," she said. Her hands were shaking and she grabbed the bottom of her sweater and held it tight. "'And—uh—I was really surprised."

Applause rippled around the room.

Katrina made an obvious effort to blink back her tears. "I don't know how to say this, but it means a lot to me that I have so many friends here at SFBA and you all went to so much trouble. I'm going to miss you so much when I leave."

With that she jumped off the chair and started to sniffle. Leah gave her a big hug and whispered, "You won't leave here. I'm not going to let you," before the rest of the kids crowded around and started to comfort her.

"Isn't Katrina silly?" Linda said to Kay a few minutes later as she handed out pieces of cake. Katrina was smiling again and joking with Raul about who should get the first slice. "She won't be leaving here for at least two years."

Leah heard Linda's comment and almost started to say something to Kay and Linda, but then she decided to keep her mouth shut. Leah didn't want to ruin Katrina's party. She put on her best smile and accepted a piece of cake from Linda.

"I really like Finola," Kay declared later that evening. The clouds had lifted and the night was mild enough for the group of girls who lived at Mrs. Hanson's boardinghouse to walk home from the Wyndhams.

"I don't know what's to like about her," Pamela Hunter commented sharply. "You don't even know her. She *seems* nice enough," Pam conceded, "but around here you don't see people's true colors until the competition gets tough."

Leah pricked up her ears at Pam's commentary and she exchanged an exasperated glance with Alex. When it came to competition, Pam was the most ruthless girl at SFBA. As far as Leah was concerned, Pam's true colors were not very attractive at all.

"It takes one to know one!" Linda said, not very quietly.

Pam whirled around and glared at Linda. Pam looked as if she were about to start a fight, but turned around and said in a loud voice to her one friend at the boardinghouse, Abigail Handhardt, "All I know about Finola is what I can see. And thank goodness she's not the same body type I am."

"No, you're not built like her at all," Abigail commented. "She's tall and very thin."

Pam's back stiffened visibly under the light of a streetlamp. "And what's that supposed to mean?" she said, coming to a dead stop and glowering at Abby.

Linda stifled a giggle and grabbed Kay's arm, then they both started to laugh. Linda and Kay were roommates, and they enjoyed sharing a double room at the boardinghouse. Kay's original roommate, Melanie Carlucci, had been accepted for an apprenticeship with the Joffrey Ballet and had left the school only a week before. Linda had been first on the list of girls waiting to get into the boardinghouse, and she had jumped at the opportunity to move nearer to the school and her friends.

"Well, it's just that she's a tall dancer," Abby explained to Pam. "She has a long back, more like—"

Abby looked back over her shoulder, then grinned "—more like Alex!"

All the girls stopped and stared at Alex.

"That's true," Pam agreed in a snide drawl. "I'm glad I'm not in your shoes, Sorokin. I know a good dancer when I see one, and I do declare Miss Darling is going to make things tough around here for you."

"You just love making trouble, don't you!" Leah snapped.

"What trouble?" Alex said nonchalantly. "I do not see Finola Darling as competition, but as someone to share parts with. I am very tired of being the tallest girl here."

"Stop being so noble," Pam said, as if the thought disgusted her. "You're perfectly capable of jealousy, Alex, and I can't wait for the fireworks when you're both fighting it out to be the Swan Queen next time there's a school production of *Swan Lake*!"

Alex just shrugged, but Leah bristled at Pam's words. Pam knew perfectly well that Leah and Alex's friendship had gone through a couple of rough patches—all because Leah managed to get roles that usually would have landed easily in Alex's lap before Leah had arrived at SFBA. Once Leah had been picked to dance Juliet with Alex's old partner James in a dance demonstration program that toured area high schools. More recently, Leah had been chosen over Alex—and Pam—to dance with Andrei Levintoff in the school gala. Since Alex had been in love with Andrei at the time, Leah's friendship with her had suffered greatly. Now that everything was back to normal, Pam was trying to stir things up again.

"We're talking about Finola so much," Suzanne

Winters finally broke in, obviously trying to change the subject, "that you would have thought it was her birthday party tonight and not Katrina's. It was weird the way she started crying when she gave that speech."

"Stage fright," Abby suggested.

"Don't be ridiculous," Pam sneered. "Frankly, I'd cry, too, if someone threw me a surprise party and I walked in dressed like that!"

"I think Katrina looked great!" Kay said, turning up the collar of her pea coat against a sudden gust of wind.

"Well, from now on I'm going to wear my best clothes on my birthday—just in case," Pam vowed, smoothing the fabric of her tan suede miniskirt. "You never know when someone will throw you a big bash."

Under her breath Leah muttered, "Fat chance." Alex elbowed Leah in the ribs and laughed silently so that Pam couldn't hear her.

"Suzanne's right, you know," Linda said. "Katrina's crying struck me as sort of silly at the time, but it's too bad the surprise party affected her that way."

"It's not the party. Something else is bothering her," Alex said. "I'm sure of that."

Leah stared down at the wet pavement a moment, then made up her mind. "Well, I guess it's no secret anymore. Katrina said that herself."

"What secret, Leah?" Kay wanted to know.

"You know she's been blue all week."

"Tell me about it!" Linda commented. "But I thought it was because we did such a good job at pretending we didn't care about her birthday."

"Her birthday has nothing to do with it." Leah chose her next words carefully, not wanting to make Katrina's situation seem worse than it really was. "She got a letter from home, and her parents have to sell their business—you know, the inn?"

"Wow! That must be tough," Linda sympathized.

"That's not all of it," Leah said. "She can't come back here next semester because her family won't be able to afford the tuition."

A shocked silence settled over the group. To Leah's surprise, even Pam looked sobered by the news. "So that explains her homemade clothes and why she never spends any money. She's poor," Pam said, sounding as if being poor were the worst thing on earth.

"There's nothing wrong with being poor," Linda snapped. "Not everyone has an easy time coming here, Pamela Hunter."

"I didn't say they did," Pam defended herself.

"Are they just temporary, these problems?" Alex asked.

"For her parents, yes," Leah replied. "But for Katrina, no. Leaving SFBA now means giving up being a dancer. Let's face it."

"Isn't there something someone like Madame Preston can do? What about Mrs. Wyndham? She's rich. I bet she'd help Katrina," Kay said.

"Katrina would never ask Mrs. Wyndham for help," Linda said with such certainty that Leah's heart sank. "It's one thing to get a scholarship, or to have the school make some long-term arrangement for payment, but it's quite another to have someone just give you a check for tuition because you're poor."

"But there is a scholarship!" Leah finally said. "And Katrina has a good chance of winning, I think."

"You mean the Louise Adams Scholarship?" Alex sounded skeptical.

"No one's ever told me about the scholarship!" Pam complained.

"The notice probably just went up today," Alex said, ignoring Pam's offended tone. "You saw it this afternoon, right, Leah?"

Leah nodded. "And I told Katrina she should go for it. Finola was there. She even volunteered to help her."

"By winning it herself?" Pam scoffed.

"She can't compete," Alex said. "Neither can I. It's for American citizens, and first- and second-year students only."

"Well, that should help Katrina *some,*" Kay said. Leah glanced at her quickly. Something in Kay's voice made it sound as if she were conjuring up one of her crazy schemes. "We all have to help Katrina," Kay stated firmly. "I don't want her to have to leave."

"No, none of us do," Alex said. "And maybe with a little luck—" She cut her sentence short and the other girls continued walking, discussing the scholarship.

Leah regarded Alex, curious. "Is it a really hard scholarship to win?" she finally asked, keeping her voice very low.

"The toughest. Dancing the lead in the first big student performance of the year is not the sort of prize that is given to just anyone. And Katrina, well—" Alex broke off and wrinkled her brow. Leah didn't have to ask Alex what she was thinking: Katrina was not the strongest dancer in the school. She had a lovely, unusual quality, and would probably land a job with a respectable company when she graduated from SFBA. But she wasn't the sort of dancer to win competitions.

Leah wondered if she had made a mistake in telling Katrina she had a good chance. Maybe it would be better, after all, to approach Madame and ask for help.

"You said the ballet was *Giselle*?" Alex asked.

Leah nodded.

"That is strange. That was the Adams evening ballet last year."

"Alex, Katrina really would make a good Giselle," she said, a note of hope in her voice. "She looks the part."

"Yes, that's true," Alex concluded as they walked up the boardinghouse steps. "And suiting the role is a very big plus, let me tell you!"

Chapter 4

Two thirds of the way through class the next morning, Leah stood in the back of the Red Studio, toweling the sweat off her shoulders and trying to catch her breath. Her eyes were riveted to a dark-haired girl executing a remarkable number of fouettés in the middle of the room. The strains of the coda to the Black Swan pas de deux from act three of *Swan Lake* echoed through the studio while the dancer sprang onto the point of one foot time after time, whipping her other leg around to the side and in toward her knee again with each quick turn.

Watching the girl perform, Leah was extremely glad that Madame was not teaching this Sunday morning class. Sunday was the one day that SFBA students were not obligated to turn up at the school, but when Madame taught, every student came. Most of the Company members and many other professional dancers who lived in the Bay area usually showed up for Madame's class as well. Today Diana Chang was filling in for the school's director. Leah hated Diana's classes in general: They were too athletic and filled with the sort of combinations Leah didn't like. But class with Diana was certainly the lesser of two evils today. At least to Leah's mind. She wasn't sure she wanted Madame's first impression of Finola Darling to be this good. Leah felt guilty for thinking that way; after all, just yesterday she had wanted Finola to be her friend. But that was before she had seen her dance.

"I think one hundred twenty-one fouettés is the world record!" Kay Larkin whispered to Leah. Until today Leah had been the fouetté champ of the school, outlasting even Pam, who was usually the most athletic dancer in the class. Last week Leah had managed thirty-five fouettés without moving very far from her starting point on the floor. "What's Finola up to now?" Kay asked.

"Fifty-two, and she's not even traveling!" Michael Litvak answered in an awed voice.

Leah was a little hurt by Michael's automatic respect for Finola. Michael was usually her partner, and he had always been incredibly impressed by *her* dancing. Now his eyes were glued to Finola as if he were looking at the eighth wonder of the world. Of course, Leah was staring at Finola, too. Her performance was truly amazing.

After four or five more turns, Finola stepped off pointe, and the music stopped. Instantly the whole class burst into applause. Finola curtsied awkwardly, then scurried over to the nearest barre, where Katrina handed her a towel. As Leah watched Finola, she caught Pam's eye from across the room. The redhead was looking at her, almost gloating, and obviously trying to gauge Leah's reaction to the new class star. Under Pam's scrutiny Leah felt her cheeks grow hot, and she began applauding even louder. Her claps were the last to ring out across the room.

Diana Chang got down from her stool in the front of the classroom and nodded graciously to Finola. "That was truly impressive. It's a good thing for the rest of the girls that you won't be able to compete next week for the Adams Scholarship."

Finola looked embarrassed by the compliment and traded an awkward grin with Katrina.

"Speaking of the scholarship," Diana continued, "I need to make an announcement. I'm afraid there's been a mistake. Tom goofed again." Diana smiled and waited for the round of giggles to subside. Ever since Tom, one of the company apprentices, had started work as the school secretary, mistakes on call-board messages had become a matter of course.

Alex sidled up to Leah. "I know what she's going to say. I had a feeling—" Alex stopped as Diana went on with her announcement.

"We told him to copy last year's announcement of the scholarship, but to change the date and other important information. He forgot to change the name of the ballet—"

A few people groaned, and Leah saw Katrina grip the barre tightly with one hand.

"*Giselle,* as you older SFBA hands will remember, was last year's Adams evening ballet. This year's will be *Swan Lake,*" Diana finally said.

"Oh, no!" Katrina wailed softly. She looked helplessly at Leah, who looked blankly back at her. Leah wanted to smile at Katrina and encourage her, but the idea of Katrina being picked to dance *Swan Lake* was really crazy. Katrina was a dainty dancer, not a strong, dramatic Swan Queen. Today Katrina had only managed fifteen or sixteen fouettés. Thinking of fouettés, Leah looked at Finola again. Like Diana said, Finola would win that scholarship hands down, given the chance. Finola would beat me, too, Leah found herself thinking.

"What beats me is why they sent her here," Diana commented in the dressing room after class. She paused to check her reflection in the mirror, and Leah watched as Diana eyed herself critically, then sucked her already perfectly flat tummy in. "If Madame had a student like that, she wouldn't let her out of her sight!" She pulled out her lipstick and carefully applied a cherry-red color to her lips.

Diana was talking about Finola Darling, just like everyone else in the room except for Katrina. Katrina hadn't turned up in the dressing room yet. She and Finola had vanished together quite mysteriously the moment class was over. Leah had a hunch that after hearing the bad news about *Swan Lake,* Finola had decided to start Katrina's coaching sessions early.

"Well, like you said, at least she can't compete against us," Pam said from the corner. The southern girl was plaiting her thick hair into a French braid. "That's all I care about. After all, her future doesn't hinge on how many competitions she wins at this school."

"Yes, I'm sure that Finola's future is something none of us has to worry about," Diana said shrewdly. "She's head and shoulders above any girl her age here! I can't wait until Madame sees her in action." It seemed as if Diana looked directly at Leah when she said that. Then with a brisk wave of her hand, Diana headed for the door. "Ta-ta!" she said cheerily. "It's Sunday, and I've got a whole afternoon off, with no rehearsals, no classes, and I actually have a date!" She slammed the door behind her, and the thin partition separating the girls' changing area from the main studio shuddered.

Leah slumped back against the wall. She felt as if Diana had just slapped her in the face. Everyone in that dressing room knew Leah was currently Madame's favorite pupil, the one she had pinned her hopes on to graduate to a truly brilliant career. Leah kicked her bare foot against the bottom of her chair. She started dully at her left big toe: It was raw and red from pointe work and her bunion was throbbing. Until this very moment Leah hadn't realized exactly how much Madame's opinion of her mattered. It had made her believe in herself and think that she was special when she felt like just another dancer. Madame's praise made all the pain and hard work worth it.

Of course, Leah reminded herself, Madame had been partial to Alex before Leah came, and she still admired Alex's talent. But Leah knew that for Alex, things around SFBA just weren't the same. Alex wasn't the rising young star of the school anymore, and Leah was—or had been until now.

Leah sat up straighter. Suddenly she knew exactly what to do: she had to show Madame and Diana and everyone else at the Academy that she was just as good as Finola. Maybe she couldn't do a million fouettés, but Leah knew she would make a great Swan Queen. Until this morning she hadn't really thought about the Adams Scholarship competition apart from Katrina and her problems. Leah hadn't thought much about entering or not entering. But Finola's performance in class today, followed by Diana's comments, made it all too clear to Leah. If she wanted to remain the best dancer in the school, she had to go for that scholarship, and she had to win it. Leah grabbed her jeans and practically jumped into them. Her decision had filled her with a great deal of energy. She needed to get out of the cramped dressing room and go off somewhere to be alone.

Leah grabbed her coat off the rack and shouldered her bag.

"Hey, where are you going?" Alex asked.

"I don't know. Out."

"I thought you were coming with us to the movies," Kay said, disappointed.

"No, uh, I've got a project in the art studio to finish, and I'm way behind with my French homework again." Leah's excuse sounded a little fake, and Leah was sorry she had lied. She probably hadn't fooled her friends one bit.

Alex, Kay, and Suzanne exchanged glances. Leah pretended not to notice, but it hurt to see that they felt sorry for her because Diana had made such a big deal about Finola. A new girl had come to school, she looked like a virtual dance prodigy, and it seemed as if Leah's friends didn't believe in her anymore. Suddenly Leah wished Finola had never come to SFBA. She had a feeling that life at the Academy would never be the same.

Muttering a curt "See you all later!" Leah left the dressing room, mad and ready to prove to everyone that she was the most talented girl in the school. But halfway down the hall something in the Blue Studio caught her eye. She peered in the door's window. Finola was in the middle of the vast empty studio, wearing a pair of wool leg warmers that sagged down below her knees and a tattered pink sweatshirt over her black leotard. She was demonstrating her famous fouettés for

Katrina. Leah started to feel jealous again, but suddenly Finola stopped.

"See, love," she said, "the trick is the rhythm. Once you get that quick spring up onto pointe right, the rest is really easy. Imagine you've got a nail coming out of the toe of your shoe that keeps you from traveling across the boards." Then Finola stepped aside and Katrina came into view. Katrina looked very skeptical, but she gritted her teeth and more or less threw herself into the motion. Finola shouted encouragement whenever it looked like Katrina was about to give up. By the time Katrina had to stop, Leah had counted twenty-two of the difficult turns—more than Katrina had ever done in class before. Finola threw her arms around Katrina and her energetic voice floated out into the hallway. "I knew you could do it! Katrina Gray, you're really going to knock those judges' socks off!"

Hearing Finola's encouragement for Katrina, Leah felt very guilty. Finola was helping Katrina at the very same moment that Leah was plotting to beat her. Leah's own desire to prove she was the best dancer had made her forget how important winning the competition was to Katrina, her friend. If Leah lost, she'd still be able to study at the school. But if Leah won, Katrina's dancing days were over. The thought of what she was trying to do was so awful that Leah tore herself away from the door and flew down the steps, through the double French doors that opened on the back lawn, and out into the rain.

On the broad steps that led down to the path, Leah paused and pressed her hands to her burning cheeks. Her head was spinning and she had no idea what to do next. She looked out across the wet grass, past the gazebo, at the mist-shrouded domed building that housed the swimming pool, and at the glass and concrete art building. Leah's gaze rested a moment on the solid and inviting structure. Maybe working with clay would be just the therapy she needed to regain her concentration. She was feeling terribly off balance and out of focus, as if she weren't exactly sure who she was or what she wanted anymore. Besides, she had told her friends she had an art project to finish, and though that wasn't exactly true, hard work at the pottery studio always helped Leah put her life back in perspective again.

Leah sloshed her way through the puddles on the path, feeling almost as dismal and gray as the sky looked. The earlier downpour had tapered off to a misty drizzle, but Leah didn't bother to put her umbrella up for the short walk. Little streams of water found their way down the collar of her yellow slicker, and Leah actually took some satisfaction in getting wet and feeling miserable. She deserved to be miserable. The whole issue of competing for the scholarship confused Leah: If she didn't compete because Katrina needed to win, that would be dishonest, and unfair to Katrina. Katrina shouldn't win by default. But competing to show the faculty and her friends that she was the best dancer in the school didn't exactly feel honest to Leah either.

Leah's head was still spinning as she walked into the art studio. The light drum of rain on the skylight was a comforting sound. Leah tossed her slicker on the linoleum-surfaced counter of the pottery room and pulled a smock from the rack. Then she grabbed a chunk of clay from beneath a sheet of plastic and headed for the wedging board.

With strong, quick motions she began to knead the lump into a smooth round ball. Pounding the clay felt good to Leah, and as she wedged it, she began to let go of some tension. At least ceramics was something she was good at, and throwing pots never failed to calm her down.

Leah bypassed the electric wheels and went over to the kick wheel in the corner. Generally the girls avoided using it, because Miss Azenaro, their art teacher, had told them once it wasn't good for their knees. But Leah preferred the hard physical work involved, and at the moment she needed to vent her confusion and anger somehow. Kicking to make the wheel work was certainly better than lashing out at one of her friends.

Leah threw down her ball of clay and kicked the wheel until the clay spun round and round very fast. She cupped her hands around the small gray ball and tried to center it. For a while it seemed as if Leah's self-appointed therapy might work. She poked her fingers in the smoothly spinning small tower of clay to start a pot, but she pressed too hard with one finger and her nail broke through the wall of clay. She slowed the wheel, let out a frustrated sigh, and tossed her would-be pot into the slip bucket.

Leah got some more clay, wedged it, and threw it down on the wheel, determined to make it work this time. But her hands suddenly felt weak, and the clay seemed to have a mind of its own. The more she fought to center it, the more lopsided it got. *"Arrrrgh!"* Leah shouted into the empty studio. She grabbed the clay off the wheel which was still spinning crazily and flung it at the opposite wall. The clay stuck to the wall for a second, then slid down to the floor in a sticky, gooey mass.

"Bravo!!!"

Leah jumped. The studio had seemed deserted. "Who's there?" she asked, turning around, embarrassed that someone had witnessed her temper tantrum. Then she saw it was Andrei Levintoff, and she relaxed a little. Andrei was a good friend.

"Andrei, what are you doing here?"

"Working," Andrei answered in a heavy Russian accent. Andrei was a guest artist with the company this season and taught one repertory class a week at the school.

"How can you work here?" Leah asked, amazed at how messy the handsome young dancer looked. He was wearing a very baggy pair of old paint-spattered jeans that looked as if they once belonged to Mr. Jefferson, grounds keeper and school custodian.

"I mean my painting work, not my dance work," Andrei explained with a boyishly charming smile. With pink- and green-stained fingers he flicked a lock of his longish brown hair out of his eyes. "Come see what I make, then you tell me what this—" he waved at the mess on the floor "—this work of art is. Okay?" He reached out and took Leah's hand.

Leah blushed. Andrei's touch still made her tremble. A few weeks ago Leah had danced in the fund-raising gala with Andrei as her partner. She had received rave reviews for her performance, but she wondered what the critics would have said if they had really known why she danced "like a girl inspired." She had fallen hook, line, and sinker for Andrei, imagining he was in love with her, too. And Alex, her best friend, had thought Andrei was in love with *her*. Leah and Alex had actually fought over Andrei. Both girls had been humiliated when they learned that Andrei was engaged to another ballerina, one who lived in New York. Relations between Leah and Alex were back to normal, but around Andrei, Leah still felt embarrassed, very young, and inexperienced. She had been such a fool to believe that a nineteen-year-old ballet star could fall in love with her.

Leah followed Andrei around the corner into the painting studio, being careful to avoid knocking over the easels that were stacked against the wall.

"Do you like it?" Andrei asked.

Leah quickly located Andrei's painting on an easel in the far corner, where the light was brightest. "I love it," she said. "But I don't know what it is," she admitted honestly.

Andrei threw back his head and laughed. "It is an abstract painting. But if you look carefully, you will see it is a ballerina in a low arabesque." He pointed to a swirl of pink and muted green and gray, and though Leah couldn't quite make out the shape of the dancer, the stripes of paint gave the exact feel of the movement.

"Leah, I must ask of you a favor," Andrei said, looking at her closely. "Would you come here this week and model for me? I need someone who will fit into the Juliet costume. I hear that one time you have worn it, no?"

Leah nodded.

"I need a dancer to stand, perhaps with her hand on a chair for a while on pointe, to get the line right and the feeling of the movement," Andrei explained.

"I'd be glad to," Leah said, happy he had asked her. Then her face fell. "Except—" She paused and rubbed her dirty hands on the side of her smock. "I need to practice a lot next week. There's a big competition—for a scholarship." She felt weird saying that, as if she were lying. She wasn't really competing for the scholarship money at all, she wanted only to prove herself. "I won't have much time," she explained.

"I need only a little time. One hour maybe. I can borrow the costume for one day, Tuesday. Then it has to be cleaned for Thursday's performance at the Opera House. So is it a date? Tuesday?"

"Okay," Leah said reluctantly. She didn't want to let Andrei down.

"Now, about this mess—" Andrei put his arm around her and walked her back to the pottery room.

"Oh, I just got angry at a pot—it wouldn't work. That's all," Leah said quickly.

"I do not think you are angry at a pot. I think maybe something else is bothering you."

"What makes you say that?" Leah said. Keeping her back to Andrei, she began to clean up the mess. She scraped the wet clay off the floor and flung it into the slip bucket, where it landed with a loud splash.

"Because it is Sunday, and you are not with your friends, and you are not rehearsing. I think you are angry with someone, not clay."

"That's ridiculous," Leah protested, but she was unable to keep the color from rising to her cheeks.

"Andrei, are you still in there?" a voice called from outside the studio. A moment later Diana Chang's head poked around the corner. She looked at Andrei and Leah and raised her eyebrows, not bothering to hide her surprise at finding them together.

"Diana, what are you doing here?" Leah asked.

Diana gave Leah a hard look, and Leah lowered her eyes. She hadn't meant to antagonize the older dancer. She had enough troubles with Finola and Katrina right now, and the last thing she needed was another fallout with Diana. "I mean— you said you had a date this afternoon."

Diana pursed her lips and dusted off the top of a high stool before hoisting herself on top of it. "I do have a date in Berkeley. But I'm afraid my ride to Berkeley forget all about me!" She gave Andrei a severe look, then softened her full red lips into a pretty smile. "Where have you been?" she asked, then tapped her watch. "Danny is waiting. We're already twenty minutes late."

"Your ride!" Andrei's hand flew up to his mouth. "I forgot. I came here to paint for half an hour and the time went by and I do not notice." He was so upset with himself that his English was deteriorating with every word. "I hurry now. I change clothes. I drive you to Berkeley right away and you tell Danny to blame me, no?"

"Yes," Diana said firmly. "I'll blame you, but hurry up now, don't just stand there. Get out of those awful clothes—" She wrinkled her delicate nose. "They look like they're hand-me-downs from Mr. Jefferson."

"Yes, he give them to me to paint. A little big, but very comfortable."

Diana laughed at Andrei as he ran off toward the painting studio. A moment later they heard an easel move, some muttering in Russian, and the sound of clothes being thrown around the room.

While she waited for Andrei, Diana regarded Leah coolly. "So, I don't believe I heard *your* reaction to our new friend Finola. She's pretty good, isn't she?"

Leah had a feeling that Diana was trying to bait her. "Yes. She's one of the best dancers I've seen here, if not the best."

Diana frowned. Leah hadn't planned her words to come out like that, but she had just implied that Finola was more accomplished than Diana.

"What is Finola? I do not know that word." Andrei came out of the painting studio, his black leather coat over one arm and his car keys in one hand. With his other hand Andrei was trying to button the collar of his shirt. Diana reached up and buttoned it for him in a way that made Leah cringe. Diana knew perfectly well that Andrei was engaged, but she always flirted with him anyway.

"A Finola, Mr. Levintoff," Diana said as she playfully gave Andrei's bright red suspenders a snap, "is one of the more extraordinary things I've seen in dance."

Andrei looked bewildered.

Diana let out a sweet bell-like laugh. "She's the new exchange student from the upper school of the Royal Ballet in England. She's here for a year. Ask Leah about Finola, she saw her in class today." Diana turned to Leah, all smiles.

Leah drew in her breath. "She's a very good dancer," she said, barely able to keep her voice steady.

Andrei nodded but regarded Leah carefully. "She was in class this morning for the first time?"

"Yes," Diana said. "She did about fifty fouettés—"

"Fifty-seven." Leah corrected her in a tight voice.

"Turning on a dime, mind you. And you should see her adagio work. It puts Alexandra to shame!"

Now Andrei looked even more surprised. Alex wasn't only the best adagio dancer in the school, she was also Andrei's closest friend. They had known each other for a long time. "Hmmm. It sounds as if the regular students here now have much competition." He sounded sympathetic, and his eyes caught Leah's. Leah turned away quickly, afraid Andrei would guess what was bothering her and why she had been throwing that clay and—at whom.

"But I'm sure, as Leah will tell you, all this about Finola is old news!" Diana said briskly. She rested her hand on Andrei's arm and guided him to the door. "Besides, I'm late enough already, and it's all your fault."

When they got to the door, Andrei pulled his arm away from Diana and turned toward Leah. "When you have time we should finish our talk. About being angry at the wall." His smile was warm, but his eyes were full of concern.

"Anytime," Leah said quietly, though she wasn't sure she could talk about her feelings with Andrei or anyone else.

Diana opened the door, and she and Andrei walked out into the rain.

Andrei's voice floated back to Leah. "I use Leah as a model next week. I think she fits perfectly into your Juliet costume. This is fine, no?"

There was a long pause. "Leah, modeling for you?" Diana finally asked. She didn't say more, but Leah could tell from the tone of Diana's voice that she wasn't exactly pleased with Leah wearing her costume. Now that Finola was around, Leah finally understood Diana's intense jealousy of her as an upcoming star. It didn't feel good to have your status threatened at SFBA, it felt miserable.

Chapter 5

*That night at Mrs. Hanson's board-*inghouse, the usual Sunday potluck dinner proved to be anything but potluck. At Alex's suggestion, the girls had pooled their resources—financial and culinary—and between Alex, Suzanne, Kay, and Abby, they had created a feast of roast beef, potatoes, and several different vegetables. Pam surprised everyone with homemade biscuits and a delicious-looking peach pie. Leah volunteered to wash the dishes.

When they finally got to the pie, Alex groaned and patted her flat stomach. "Remind me not to plan such a good meal again—not the night after a birthday party."

Kay's hand flew to her mouth and she gave a despairing look at the large piece of pie on her plate. "I forgot all about that. If I eat this, I'm going to break the scale!"

"Don't be ridiculous," Linda Howe said from the dining room door. "Kay, the only scale you'll break is the one in the post office weighing enve-lopes!" Everybody laughed and Linda tossed her jacket on the hall rack. She walked into the dining room and sat down next to Leah. "Who baked this?" she asked, pulling the small remains of the pie toward her while reaching for a plate with her other hand.

"Little ol' me!" Pam drawled, beaming.

Linda looked surprised. "I never thought you were the domestic type!" Pam glared at Linda, but her expression softened when Linda took her first bite. Her eyebrows shot up with delight. "Mmmm—this is great! Next time you guys are planning pie for dessert, remind me not to go to my uncle's for dinner."

"Okay, but you promise to cook something. Having one noncook around here is quite enough." Alex turned to Leah.

Leah tried to smile, then looked down at her plate and poked her fork into her pie; she put her fork down without tasting it. Food didn't seem to have much appeal tonight. Leah leaned back in her chair and sighed.

"Hey, you don't look so good," Linda commented to Leah. "Do you feel all right?"

Alex and Kay looked at each other. Leah pursed her lips and shoved back her chair. Her friends had no doubt spent part of the afternoon talking about Leah and her reaction to seeing Finola dance. "I guess I don't," she answered. "Actually, I haven't felt right since the party last night. I had too much junk food," she lied. Leah began stacking plates to carry to the kitchen.

"Tell me about it," Linda said. "I think I ate a whole bag of potato chips. What's up with you, Kay?"

Leah stopped collecting the silverware and looked down the long dining room table at Kay.

"With me?" Kay took the last bite of her pie

and washed it down with a sip of milk. "Nothing's up. What makes you ask?"

"I thought you might have hurt yourself in class or something," Linda stated matter-of-factly. "When I dropped by school on my way back here, I noticed you'd taken your name off the list for the competition."

"What?" several voices cried in unison. All heads turned toward Kay.

"Why did you do a dumb thing like that?" Alex asked bluntly.

"Oh, I think I'd look too much like a canary dancing the Swan Queen," the short girl joked. Then she paused just long enough to get everyone's undivided attention. "Actually—it's part of my plan."

"Plan?" Leah repeated. She had a funny feeling in the pit of her stomach. Wasn't it Kay who had said something about doing everything possible to help Katrina stay in school last night?

Alex narrowed her dark eyes and studied Kay. "I have a feeling, Katherine Larkin, that you're about to drop one of your famous schemes on us."

"It's not a scheme," Kay retorted with dignity. Then she sat up a little straighter in her chair and struggled to look serious. "I figured we have to do all we can to help Katrina win this scholarship. If she doesn't win, she's out of SFBA. If I don't win—" Kay gave a nonchalant little shrug. "My pride takes one more pratfall and then I get up, dust myself off, and nothing really changes."

"So you decided not to compete to give Katrina a better chance?" Linda asked, amazed.

Leah sat down slowly and carefully placed the stack of dishes back on the table.

Kay just grinned. "You got it—and I'm going to do my best to get as many girls as I can to stay out of the competition." She rubbed her hands together and looked expectantly around the table. "Any volunteers?"

Leah's heart almost stopped beating. The other girls were probably going to hop on Kay's bandwagon to save Katrina. If Leah didn't, what would her friends think of her? Competing for the scholarship would seem like competing against Katrina.

Alex drummed her fingers on the table, then leaned back in her chair. She brushed a fleck of lint off her jet-black turtleneck and shook her head slowly. "I do not like this plan."

"What's it to you?" Pam said archly. "You can't compete anyway."

"It's not fair to Katrina, that's why," Alex stated firmly.

Kay balked. "What's unfair about it, Alex?"

"It makes it seem as if without interfering—that is not the word—" Alex looked to Leah for help.

It took a moment, but Leah finally found her voice. "You mean it's like fixing an election—something like that." Once Leah uttered the idea aloud, she was glad she had come up with a reason to say no to Kay's plan. Fixing elections was wrong, and rigging competitions was wrong, too.

Alex's high-cheekboned face brightened. "Yes, that's it. And maybe Katrina could win this prize *without* your help, Kay."

"But just last night you sounded pretty skeptical about Katrina's chances—and that's when we all thought the ballet was *Giselle*," Abigail pointed out.

"I know that," Alex conceded, "and she will

have a tough time. But it—it just seems very wrong to me."

"It doesn't to me," Suzanne said. "I'll volunteer to take my name off the list, first thing tomorrow."

Abby flashed Kay a timid smile. "Before class I'll cross my name off, too."

Linda shook her head. "No." She gave an apologetic shrug. "Kay's idea is really generous, but I can't afford not to at least try for the scholarship. My uncle took out a loan to send me here, and it just wouldn't be fair to him if I gave up."

Kay grabbed Linda's arm. "You're absolutely right. And I think that anyone who needs the money should go for it." Kay and Linda traded smiles, and then both of them turned to Leah.

Leah shrank back in her chair. "I—I—" She couldn't tell them why she had to compete, but she also couldn't lie. "I don't know what I'm going to do yet."

Disappointment registered on Kay's round, freckled face. "What do you mean, Leah? You already have the Golden Gate Award, and your mom seems to be managing the rest of the tuition."

"But it's hard for her," Leah protested, feeling a bit dishonest. It *was* hard for her mother, and it would help to have a scholarship to make up the difference between the small stipend attached to the Golden Gate prize and the high SFBA tuition. But without the extra money, Leah could still come to school. Money wasn't the reason Leah was going to try for the scholarship, Finola was.

"Come off it, Stephenson," Pam said suddenly. "I know what you're going to do. The same thing I'm going to do. Leah, the great Stephenson, is born to compete. She wants to be a star, just like I do. And the only way to get to the top is to go for that brass ring every time." Pam's tone was sarcasatic, even taunting, yet she spoke with a passion Leah had never seen in her before. Looking at Kay with unveiled contempt, she declared, "*I* for one did not come to this school to make things easier for Katrina Gray. I came here to be the best ballerina there is, and nothing and no one is going to stop me. Being noble sounds good, but I think it's more important to win. It's not tuition that's at stake here. It's a career."

Pam shoved back her chair and got up. "Leah knows all about that. Why don't you ask her what she *really* thinks about throwing this competition in Katrina's favor? Beneath that sugar-and-spice golden-girl exterior, Leah's a fighter." Pam tossed her mane of red curls off her face and looked around the table at each girl in turn.

Leah cringed. Pam had sized her up perfectly. How did Pam know her so well? How did Leah ever end up being on the same side as the one student in SFBA that she really despised?

Kay stood up and said with great dignity, "Leah is quite capable of speaking for herself, you know." She turned to Leah with an encouraging smile on her face.

Leah swallowed hard. She toyed with the dinner napkin in her hand and finally looked up. She could barely stand looking Kay in the eye. "I'm sorry, Kay. I don't think you're right about this. I can't not compete for that scholarship."

Pam laughed in triumph, then gathered the dishes from her end of the table and paraded to the kitchen.

Kay stared at Leah, too stunned to speak. "I can't believe you'd do this to Katrina!"

"Kay," Alex warned, "you mean well. But I think

Leah has as much a right to compete for the Adams Scholarship as you have not to. It is up to each one of you."

Kay looked at Alex, then propped her chin on her hands. "I hadn't thought of it like that," she conceded. "Maybe Alex is right, Leah. But you have till tomorrow to think about it. You can still change your mind, you know." She paused, then brightened considerably. "Now I'm going to start calling around and get as many other girls as I can to drop out."

Kay went over to Mrs. Hanson's old-fashioned writing desk, opened the top drawer, and pulled out a piece of paper. "All the boardinghouse and host home numbers are listed here. Anyone want to help me make calls?" Abigail and Suzanne quickly volunteered.

As the three girls trooped out to use the hall phone, Alex looked as if she were lost in thought. She stood up and dusted some crumbs off her black stretch pants. She started to help Leah finish gathering the dishes. "I wonder what Madame is going to think about this!" she mused.

"You won't tell her!!!" Linda gasped, pushing the kitchen door open with her hip.

Alex looked insulted. "Of course not! I will not have to, though," she added. "She is going to wonder why the competition list is suddenly so small. Madame should have been a fortune-teller, I think sometimes. She has a way of figuring out things like this that is positively scary."

At the sink Leah turned the water on full force and squeezed in some dish detergent. While the sink filled, she turned around and looked at Alex. "Maybe she'll make everyone compete," Leah commented, hoping it was true.

"She cannot do that," Alex said. "Auditioning for a private scholarship is not compulsory here."

"No," Leah said, dejected. "I guess not."

Alex gave Leah a quizzical look, then lowered her voice and said, "You have a right to compete for it. Every first- and second-year girl here has. Kay means well, but . . ." Alex's voice trailed off. She shrugged and began drying the plates Leah handed to her.

Leah knew that Alex was trying to make her feel better about the scene in the dining room. She was also trying to give Leah a chance to confide—like Andrei had that afternoon. But Leah didn't want to start talking about her feelings. She was afraid that Alex wouldn't understand how she felt about Finola. Leah sighed. "I just wish Kay hadn't made me feel as if I were competing *against* Katrina," she said softly. "I don't want her to leave either."

Chapter 6

"Will Madame Preston teach morning class tomorrow?" Finola asked Leah before they headed into the noisy school auditorium. It was Monday morning, time for SFBA's monthly assembly. The crowded hallway smelled of wet slickers, and Leah had to press herself back against the wall to dodge someone's folding umbrella. "I was disappointed that Diana taught again today." Finola frowned and shook her head. "Her class is too athletic." She looked up quickly as if to gauge Leah's reaction to her criticism. "It's not that I don't like *her*, of course."

Leah wondered exactly what there was about Diana or her class for Finola not to like. Today Diana had done nothing but admire Finola's jump: Finola's elevation was as high as Pam's, yet she had Katrina's light, airborne quality. Quite a combination, Leah thought to herself. If she were in Finola's shoes, she'd be more than happy to take her daily dose of praise from Diana Chang. "Diana seems pleased with your work," Leah commented, hoping she sounded neutral enough.

Finola shrugged and tucked a stray strand of

wavy black hair back up into the tight braid on top of her head. "Yes, but she doesn't care if you're an artist." Finola looked right into Leah's suspicious blue eyes. "You, for instance, you are an artist."

Leah felt her whole body tighten. She had learned to seldom trust the praise of her peers at SFBA— except possibly Alex or Kay.

"She doesn't pay any attention to you in class—as if by ignoring you she can make you go away," Finola went on.

Leah's mouth dropped open. "What makes you say that?" she blurted out, stunned by Finola's uncanny diagnosis of the situation.

"I've had teachers like that." She looked Leah up and down and smiled at her ruefully. "I'm afraid I'm jealous of you, you know. I'd give anything for your quality, Leah, the way the music seems to come not from the piano when you dance, but from somewhere inside you."

Leah blushed at the compliment. Finola hadn't been trying to make up for something, or make her feel better, or subtly put her down the way some of the other girls did when they commented on each other's dancing. She had hit on just the thing that Madame and everyone else said made Leah an exceptional dancer. Considering how Leah was feeling about Finola at the moment, she felt she didn't deserve the exchange student's praise. She looked away and wondered what had become of the Leah Stephenson who once upon a time would have found it easy to say, "I'm jealous of you, too." Laughing at being jealous of someone was something Leah could no longer do; she had to be the best at everything.

After a moment Finola continued. "I want to study with Madame. She will make me an artist.

Technique is not what I need to work on. I had a teacher in Bath, where I grew up, who thought technique was everything. When I got to the Royal Ballet School, they told me I looked like I belonged in a circus, not in the ballet!" Finola let out a hearty laugh, and Leah couldn't help but smile back. "So you see," she concluded, "that's why I can't wait to begin working with Madame." Finola hugged a stack of brand new textbooks to her chest and beamed. "One year with Madame will change my life." She gave Leah a chummy nudge. "I think being away from home and here in America is going to change a lot of things, don't you, love?"

Leah tried to smile at Finola. "Yes—of course. And Madame is a great teacher." For a moment Leah paused to remember her first class with the formidable Madame Preston. It had been an audition class, and Leah had left it feeling as if she were floating ten miles above the ground. She had been convinced that even if she didn't get into the school, one session with Madame had changed her dancing forever. Now Leah was more concerned with Madame's favorable opinion of her dancing. She wondered what would happen once the school director finally did get to teach Finola. Would she ever notice Leah's quality again?

Leah glanced at Finola, who was waiting patiently for Leah to answer her question. "Madame personally supervises the training of all the SFBA girls, so she teaches morning class herself every day but Sunday, and once a month on Sundays. But sometimes she's not here, or like today when we have assembly, she has other things to do," Leah added.

Leah expected Finola to move away, but she

continued to stand next to Leah as she surveyed the crowd inside the auditorium. "What's Kay up to?" Finola asked, sounding perplexed.

Leah looked into the auditorium and spotted Kay instantly. She was in the middle of a circle of first- and second-year students: Mia Picchi, Susie Lord, Lindsay Kohlmeier, and a few girls Leah knew only by sight. From the way she was talking, Leah knew Kay was still campaigning to get them to drop out of the competition for the Adams Scholarship.

Leah wondered why Finola seemed to be in the dark about Kay's plan. "Didn't she phone you last night?" As soon as Leah asked the question, she knew the answer: Of course not. Finola wasn't eligible for the scholarship to begin with. Moreover, it was probably better if Katrina's housemate didn't know about the scheme.

"No, she didn't phone me," Finola said. "But she's been pretty mysterious all day, at least whenever I'm around. Is she planning something else to celebrate Katrina's birthday? You know I would never tell Katrina about it. Anyway, I couldn't even if I wanted to—she's off to the dentist. She's got an abscessed tooth," Finola explained. "Not exactly the break she needed before this big competition."

"No—" Leah said haltingly. She averted her eyes from Finola's. "It's pretty rotten luck, if you ask me." As for Kay, Leah knew she could never tell Finola what Kay was really up to. "I wouldn't be surprised if Kay doesn't have another surprise for Katrina in store," she said. "She feels sorry for Katrina—you know, because of her parents and all." Leah had a feeling that wasn't so far from the truth: Katrina certainly would be surprised if she knew what Kay was doing. "She must have just dreamed up a plan because she hasn't told me a thing."

Leah checked her Betty Boop watch and pretended to be horrified. "Assembly's starting any minute now, and I forgot something downstairs in my locker. I'll see you later!" She waved over her shoulder and bolted down the hall.

"I'll save you a seat!" Finola shouted after her.

In the hope that Finola would think she hadn't heard about the seat, Leah didn't look back. She hurried around the corner toward the back stairs. Halfway down she stopped and leaned against the wall, just to catch her breath and kill enough time to make her fake errand believable. Avoiding Finola didn't make her feel good, but she couldn't bear to sit next to her during Madame's assembly. Acting like Finola's friend right now seemed two-faced.

Leah absently ran her finger along the edge of a niche in the wall. She had never been two-faced before, and it made her feel more like Pam than herself. Leah wondered if perhaps she really did have something in common with Pam. The thought horrified Leah: She detested Pam. But Pam hadn't been lying when she said that Leah wanted to be a star and that she was too much a fighter to back down from competing for the Adams Scholarship—just like Pam.

That was the trouble with Pam, Leah thought. She was the meanest, most self-centered person Leah had ever met, but she was also very perceptive. Leah now knew how important getting to the top was to her, whatever the cost. If a girl like Katrina happened to be in her way, too bad. Leah hated that picture of herself and wished she could somehow erase it, but it was accurate. Leah brushed the dirt from touching the wall off her hand and started back up the stairs. The chorus of voices from the auditorium greeted her and she stepped into the hall, glad the assembly hadn't yet started.

She peeked around the corner. Finola had abandoned her post by the door. Leah stepped into the spacious hall just as Madame Preston walked onto the stage, wearing a gray silk blouse and a dusty-rose-colored suit that matched the walls perfectly. Instantly the room fell silent, and Leah slipped into the nearest empty seat. Madame proceeded to the podium, her slender back erect and her low-heeled gray pumps making a clicking sound against the bare floorboards. She stepped up to the lecture stand, put down her papers, and poked nervously at her softly upswept hair.

Madame pushed aside the microphone and spoke directly to the audience, her resonant voice easily filling the spacious chamber. "I have several important announcements to make," she began.

"First of all, I'm afraid this awful stretch of rainy weather has taken its toll on the grand old building." She looked out across the audience and smiled a tight apologetic smile. "Thus, we will all be somewhat inconvenienced until the rain stops, and until some repairs are made. For those of you who have not been up to the third floor yet today, the roof is leaking very badly, and in the West Studio a piece of the ceiling fell in while a couple of Company members were rehearsing early this morning. Fortunately, no one was hurt. But I am told that the rest of the top-floor studios are just not safe until we get the roof fixed and the ceilings replastered. So until further notice, the entire third floor is off limits to anyone but the custodial staff and other workmen."

The whole audience groaned and Madame quickly held up her hand. "The timing on this couldn't have been worse, but there's no sense complaining about it. With the Adams Scholarship competition coming up in a few days, and the Company just into the first week of its season, rehearsal space was already at a premium. We are all going to have to make do with what little space is available to use now. The scholarship contestants will pick up rehearsal schedules when they leave the auditorium. Your practice time will be limited—"

Another ripple of complaints went around the room. Madame tapped the podium with her pencil and glared out over the audience until it fell silent. Then she softened her stern expression. "The judges will take that into consideration. If you have read the notices on the call-board, you already know that every judge is familiar with each girl's work, so everything won't hinge entirely on your performance on Wednesday." Madame paused and flipped through her papers. "The next problem is that the refurbishing of this auditorium has been scheduled to start tomorrow. Which means that the scholarship competition must be moved to another location. As the Company is rehearsing on the Opera House stage, we cannot have the competition there, and our second-floor studios are booked for rehearsals." Madame smoothed her hair back from her face and let out a sigh. "We are currently looking for a suitable space, and I am sure something will turn up by Wednesday. But it is every contestant's responsibility to check the call-board Wednesday morning to see where the contest will be, as well as what transportation arrangements have been made, if transportation should prove necessary."

A few seats away Lindsay Kohlmeier whispered to Suzanne, "This whole competition is beginning to feel jinxed!"

Leah couldn't have agreed more. She found it hard to imagine anything more unsettling than not knowing where you were supposed to compete. She would have to dance her best on the surface of a stage she'd never even laid foot on before. Worse yet, private practice space and time were going to be severely limited. Leah slumped down on her chair and wondered if it was worth competing at all.

Madame pushed aside her paper and took off her silver-rimmed glasses. Again she scanned the audience, slowly and with great deliberation. Leah shrank back under her gaze. It was as if even from that great distance, she was peering intently into each girl's very soul. "A very curious matter has come to my attention. The Louise Adams Scholarship is perhaps the biggest competitive opportunity of the year. Yet very few eligible students have signed up, and many have crossed their names off the list." Madame stopped. Leah noticed that every girl in the room kept staring straight ahead, not looking at one another at all.

After a long silence Madame Preston continued. "The poor turnout is a great disappointment to me and to the rest of the faculty. I cannot fathom what is going on here. I would like to remind you that winning the scholarship is not just an honor but provides one of the few opportunities for a junior student to dance the lead in a full-length ballet. Of course, participation in the competition is not compulsory. But I hope that those of you who have not signed up yet will seriously reconsider your reasons for holding back."

Madame made a few more routine announcements: about the cafeteria, academic grades, and upcoming performance opportunities with local dance groups. Then the assembly was over.

Though Leah was right by the rear door, she hung back in her seat, waiting for the crowd to thin. Kay went by, then Linda, and Alex with Finola in tow. Finola looked at Leah and mouthed, "Where were you?"

Leah tapped her watch and mouthed back, "Late."

Finola waved a scolding finger at Leah, then smiled and turned back to her conversation with Alex. Leah made her way down the row of seats into the aisle. She was almost the last girl to leave. Madame had posted herself at the door, and she was handing out rehearsal schedules. When Leah approached, Madame handed her two schedules.

"Leah, please give this second schedule to Katrina. She won't be back at school until this afternoon, and I'm afraid if I post it on the callboard she'll miss it."

"Sure," Leah said. She folded both sheets and stuffed them in the outside zipper compartment of her dance bag.

"I'm very pleased to see that you, at least, have not taken your name off the competition list," Madame said. "Do you know why so many of the girls have changed their minds about competing?" Madame Preston's steel-gray eyes seemed to hypnotize Leah, and for a second she felt as if she were about to tell Madame the whole story—

about Katrina's dilemma, Kay's well-meant effort—everything except her envy of Finola. But out of the corner of her eye she caught Kay staring at her and frowning. Leah carefully positioned herself where she didn't have to look at Kay. If Leah did tell Madame what was going on, the school director might find another way to help Katrina, that way the contest wouldn't be so crucial to Katrina's future. But telling the truth would be ratting on her friends. Leah was sure she could never live with herself if she did that.

"I don't know, Madame," Leah finally answered, trying to look innocent. "Really, I don't."

Madame held her gaze a moment, then pursed her lips. "All right. Don't forget to give the schedule to Katrina."

"I won't," Leah said, and hurried down the hall, grateful to see that Kay and the other girls were already gone. When she rounded the corner with her head down, she ran right into Andrei.

Andrei let out a gasp of surprise, then held Leah at arm's length and smiled warmly. "Just the girl I want to see!"

A group of girls came down the hall and stared frankly at Andrei and Leah standing so close. Leah pulled her arm away from his hand and stepped out of their view into a little alcove near the stairs.

"Today not Tuesday I am able to borrow the Juliet costume!" Andrei announced. "I just found out they will need it back tomorrow night at the Opera House. So can you model for me this afternoon? Maybe around four."

Leah looked blankly at Andrei. She had been so preoccupied with her own problems that she'd forgotten all about her promise to pose for his painting. "Four o'clock? Okay," she said without giving it much thought. "But I have to run now or I'll be late for French!" Andrei waved good-bye and Leah ran down the long hall of the modern academic wing. She had already forgotten about Andrei: She was back to thinking about the problem of limited practice time before Wednesday's competition. Would she have enough time to prepare, Leah wondered.

Chapter 7

"Madame Preston has some nerve!"
Pamela Hunter grumbled, setting her tape recorder
down on the dressing room bench. "If more people actually *had* signed up for the scholarship
competition, no one would have been able to
rehearse anyway." She peeled off her sweaty leotard and reached for a towel. "I think they'd be
better off just postponing the whole thing."

It was almost three o'clock and Leah was in
front of the mirror, struggling to pull her abun-
dant blond hair into a tight ponytail. For the third
time in five minutes, the elastic broke. Leah threw
the remains of the rubber band against the wall
and sat down on the bench. "Nothing about this
competition is going right, nothing," she complained. She propped her chin on her hands and
her hair fell forward, covering most of her face.

Pam looked up from a cloud of talcum powder.
"Things going that badly?" To Leah's amazement,
Pam didn't sound as if she were gloating. She
actually sounded interested.

Leah looked up and pushed her hair back from
her eyes. Pam reached in her bag and handed

Leah a terry-cloth po tail tie. "Is it your re-hearsal time now?" she asked. "Did you get just one hour today and a half hour tomorrow like me?" Pam sounded a little suspicious, as if Leah might have somehow been awarded extra practice time because Madame favored her.

"Yes," Leah answered, glad to hear the hostility back in Pam's voice. For a moment there she had almost confided in her. Unfortunately, if anyone understood competitiveness at SFBA, it was the Atlanta-born redhead: Pam would understand Leah's need to prove herself because of Finola. But Leah knew she couldn't trust Pam. If Pam found out what was really motivating Leah to compete, she would use it against her—somehow, someday. That was Pam's way. Leah went back to the mirror and managed to secure her ponytail without further mishap. She wrapped her hair around into a very tight topknot and pushed some bobby pins in tight to hold it.

The clock struck three just as Leah ran out of bobby pins. She patted her hair and quickly checked her reflection in the mirror. "I can't talk now," she said to Pam. "Like you said, there's little enough rehearsal time as it is!"

Leah walked into the Green Studio, hoping her friend Robert, the accompanist, hadn't let her down. She had pleaded with him to hang around school after repertory class and play for her.

Robert was there, and the empty, spacious room was inviting. Some of the tension went out of Leah's shoulders. This competition wasn't really jinxed. Everything would be all right once she started dancing.

"I'm glad you stayed to play for me," Leah said to Robert, putting one hand on the shiny black surface of the Steinway as she did some warm-up pliés.

"How can I resist those big blue eyes?" Robert said jokingly. He was a piano and composition major at the conservatory, and a good friend of Alex's and Leah's. Robert always encouraged Leah about her dancing. With his help, and a lot of carefully selected books from the school library, Leah was filling in her own all too sketchy knowledge of music.

Leah finished her pliés and did a few loose-swinging battements en cloche. Then she stretched out her back and asked Robert if he knew the music for Odette's solo in the second act of *Swan Lake.* He produced the ballet score with a flourish. "Since the Adams Scholarship Evening Ballet will be *Swan Lake,* I came prepared," he said. "Last year the girls didn't have to dance a solo for the judges, though," he commented as Leah walked to a corner of the studio to take her position.

"I don't know that they will for sure on Wednesday," Leah said as she tried to remember the opening combination. "But I want to practice the one or two bits I already know so that I'll feel more like a swan—and in case they ask for combinations drawn from the ballet's actual choreography."

Robert nodded and started the music. Leah tentatively performed the first few steps of the solo. It was one of her favorite pieces, and she, Alex, and Lindsay had studied it the week before in repertory class. It always helped Leah if she pretended she was in costume; it made the music move her more dramatically. Most teachers insisted that the girls be able to dance to the count of the beat, with no music. And sometimes Madame made them do half a barre with only the rhythmic one-two-three-four clap of her hands. But for Leah, music was the heart of her dancing, and picturing herself in the fluffy white tutu with a feather headdress and a sparkling crown actually helped her remember the steps and dance them better.

The practice session started out well. The Tchaikovsky melodies seemed to erase all Leah's worries about Katrina, the competition, and Finola. Leah worked through the first section of the solo several times. The actual choreography suited Leah. She loved the expansive feeling of the sissonnes, and the arabesques with the slightly bent raised leg that were somewhere between an arabesque and an attitude. One witty English ballerina had once dubbed them "attibesques," Leah remembered. Leah didn't even bother to look in the mirror. She wanted simply to concentrate on the steps and the shape of the whole passage as she moved from one corner of the room forward. The music seemed to fill her body, and her arms actually began to feel like wings. Unlike most dancers, Leah hated working with mirrors. She supposed that was something she had inherited from her teacher, Hannah Greene, back at home in San Lorenzo. Miss Greene had often said that dancers became too dependent on watching their reflections: Not only did their constantly turned heads detract from the line of the steps they were doing, but it gave them no sense of dancing on stage, where, of course, there was no mirror at all except in the eyes of the audience.

But the fourth time Leah went through the first portion of the solo, she decided to check her reflection. At first she enjoyed making small corrections in the tilt of her head, the height of her raised leg, or the backward sweeping movement of her arms. But the more Leah watched herself, the more apparent the flaws in her dancing became. There was something a little stiff, and not at all swanlike in her movement. Leah struggled to make herself look the way the music felt to her: expansive, supple, yearning, and afraid.

All at once Leah dropped off pointe and stomped to the middle of the room, her hands on her hips. Robert's music went on for a few more bars, then stopped. The room was silent except for the scuff of Leah's toe shoe as she rubbed it absently against the wood floor.

"You want to pick up again, from just after the sissonnes?" Robert asked.

"Why bother!" Leah retorted sharply. When she turned to face the piano her cheeks were red and her eyes glistened with tears. "I'm never going to get this scholarship. Never!" She walked over and leaned on the wall next to the open window. The cool damp breeze was bad for her warmed-up muscles, but she didn't care.

Leah heard Robert walk over and stand behind her. "Is something wrong, Leah?" He sounded perplexed. Leah knew Robert worked with all sorts of students and members of the Company and was sensitive to their moods. He also knew that Leah was generally not the temperamental sort. She almost never let herself get angry at her performance, or the accompanist, or the choreography.

"I wish people would stop asking me that!" she snapped, and walked over to the corner to get her towel. She slung it over her shoulders and walked up to the mirror. Studying her reflection,

Leah tried to make her arms move like wings. There was a famous tape in the library of the great Russian ballerina Maya Plisetskaya dancing the White Act of *Swan Lake.* As she exited the stage at one point, her arms seemed to change into actual wings, with the air rippling over them. Every girl at SFBA had tried to achieve that effect, but the only one who ever came close was Alex. Kay said it was Alex's supple Russian back, the result of her early training at the Vaganova Institute. Whatever it was, Leah sure didn't have it. Alex should be the Swan Queen, Leah thought to herself. That would solve everything. She could deal with Alex being better than she was, but not Finola.

Leah blew out an exasperated breath and sprang back onto pointe. She tossed the towel into the corner and bourréed around so that she was facing Robert. "We might as well take it from the top," she said in a defeated voice.

Robert cocked his head and peered at Leah over the top of his glasses. He seemed about to protest, then he shrugged and returned to the piano for the beginning of the solo.

This time the sissonnes were stiff and Leah's hop onto pointe was jerky. Instead of stopping, she forced herself to go on. She stabbed at the floor with her foot and practically wrenched her back as she tried to make her arabesque look longer and more elegant. Again she fell off pointe.

"Hi there. Need some help?" Finola's crisp voice cut through the stuffy atmosphere of the studio like a beam of light.

Leah whirled around, shocked to see the English dancer. Finola was in her street clothes, obviously on her way home. She favored Leah with a smile and tossed her dance bag into the corner. "Those sissonnes in the beginning are a tricky lot, aren't they?"

She stepped in front of Leah and squeezed her feet into a perfect fifth position. "Could you start the music again?" she asked Robert with a smile.

When the music started, she pulled herself up and began the first combination of steps. Leah watched with a crazy mixture of emotions. No, Finola wasn't Russian or Russian-trained, and her back was nothing like Alex's, but she looked wonderful doing the familiar steps. In spite of her black stretch pants and funky green sweater, she looked as regal and birdlike as any Swan Queen should. Part of Leah studied Finola's movement hoping to copy her, to try to mimic her technique and fluid style. But another part of Leah was furious: What right did Finola have to barge in on her, on her own practice time, and play coach? Finola was only a year older than Leah, and she wasn't that much more of an experienced dancer. As soon as Finola got halfway through the variation, she stopped, and Robert stopped playing as well.

"Thank you for the demonstration," Leah said in a cold, formal tone.

Finola looked at her, puzzled. "Was that a help?" she asked uncertainly.

"It was very nice, thank you, but I really don't need your help." Leah stood very straight and walked over to the barre. She grabbed her leg warmers and put them on with quick, angry gestures. "In case you didn't hear, practice time is very limited. I can't really afford to waste it, not now." Leah put her hands on her hips and stared at Finola then pointedly shifted her gaze to the door.

"Oh, I'm terribly sorry," Finola said, walking to the corner to pick up her bag. "I was only trying to help." She looked hard at Leah, and her gray eyes seemed to flicker beneath the lights as if they were filling up with tears. "I'll leave now." With one last confused look toward Leah, Finola rushed out of the room.

Leah stomped back toward the mirror and folded her arms across her chest. Her throat suddenly felt constricted, as if she were about to cry, too. Why had she been so mean to Finola? She was only trying to help. But Leah didn't want her help: It was bad enough seeing that Finola was a better dancer than she was. Leah could never live with the notion that she had won the contest with Finola's help. She felt bad about being rude to Finola, but not as bad as she had felt watching Finola sail through those steps, in her boots and pants and sweater, looking more the Swan Queen than Leah ever could even if she were wearing the costume.

"Do you want to go on?" Robert asked in a timid voice.

"Of course I want to go on," Leah said in an angry tone. She went back to her starting corner without meeting Robert's eyes. She focused her gaze above his head and the music started. But halfway through the second pair of sissonnes, Leah slipped. "Darn!" she cried as her leg crumbled underneath her.

Robert was at her side instantly. "Are you all right?" he rubbed her back gently with his hand.

Leah nodded, staring at the floor. "I'm fine, really I am." To prove the point, she stood up and carefully rubbed her left knee. It was sore, and it would be black and blue tomorrow, but it felt fine. "Let's go on," she urged.

Leah walked back to her starting point one more time, but Robert didn't move. "No, Leah," he said hesitantly. "You're too upset."

"I am *not* upset," she said through gritted teeth.

"You are, too! You're attacking your dancing as if you're trying to hurt yourself—or someone else. I don't know"—Robert shrugged and threw his hands up in the air—"but you aren't dancing like the Leah Stephenson I know. You should stop now before you get hurt."

Leah was about to argue, when the studio door squeaked open. It was a second-year student named Barbara that Leah knew only by sight and had never really spoken to.

"Sorry, Leah, your time is up," Barbara mumbled apologetically. With one finger she pointed at the clock. It was two minutes to four. Leah was about to protest that she had two more minutes to go, but Robert had already collected his music and he was headed for the studio door. "See you tomorrow," he called.

"In the small studio behind the office," Leah called out. Robert lifted his hand in a wave and closed the door behind him.

Leah scurried to the corner as Barbara plugged in her tape player. "I'll be out in a minute," Leah grumbled. All of a sudden she remembered she was supposed to model for Andrei at four o'clock. "Oh, no," she murmured under her breath. "Whatever made me say I'd do that!" She hurried to the dressing room, and five minutes later she was back in her street clothes and running down the stairs.

Leah pushed open the French doors leading out to the yard and bumped right into Katrina. Katrina's right cheek was swollen and her eyes were puffy. She looked so terrible that Leah almost didn't recognize her as they stood staring at each other a moment, startled, on the back steps.

"Katrina, you look awful!" Leah exclaimed, then clapped her hand over her mouth.

"I know," Katrina said, sounding miserable. Her face seemed to be frozen in a permanent frown. She could hardly open her mouth, and her words came out in a blurred mumbled. "Mrs. Wyndham told me to just go home and sleep, but I have to pick up some books first. Then I'm going to Mrs. Hanson's. Kay promised to help me with my homework."

Leah nodded. "I'll see you later then. I've got to run now. I promised Andrei I'd model for him over in the studio."

Katrina tried to smile. "That sounds like fun," she said between half-closed lips.

"I can't say I'm looking forward to it, but I promised." Leah stood there a minute trying to think of something that would make Katrina feel better.

"Don't worry," Katrina assured her. "The dentist said I'll be able to eat by dinner. And someday I will smile again," she concluded with remarkably good cheer.

Leah waved good-bye and ran out into the rain and the wind. She splashed through the puddles on the path leading toward the art building. Just past the gazebo Leah stopped dead in her tracks. She whirled around, hoping to catch a glimpse of Katrina's green plastic rain jacket, but Katrina had already vanished. "Rats!" Leah said out loud.

"The schedule!" She had forgotten to give Katrina her copy of the revised practice schedule. She hesitated a moment, wondering if she should run back to the main building to look for her friend. Then the clock in the tower of the nearby church chimed a quarter past four. She was already late for her appointment with Andrei. Leah continued on to the studio, jogging down the slippery path. She'd see Katrina later that night at the boarding-house. She could pass along the schedule then.

Chapter 8

A paintbrush sailed through the air and landed just inches from Leah's feet. Leah jumped. "Hey, what do you think you're doing?"

Andrei grabbed a handful of brushes from an old coffee tin and tossed them noisily onto the table. He glared at Leah again, then stomped over to the window and studied the rain.

Leah rolled her eyes up to the skylight and rubbed her bare upper arms. The kilns in the pottery room next door were off and the art studio was freezing. She was wearing Diana Chang's skimpy Juliet costume, which was little more than a spaghetti-strap nightgown. And if Andrei managed to get paint on it, Diana would have Leah's head.

"You don't have to throw things at me," Leah complained in a petulant voice.

Andrei whirled around. "Leah," he started in an exasperated, very loud voice, "I ask you small favor, no? I say one hour for one day please come here to the studio and stand still." Andrei paused. Leah could tell that he was furious. "But no. You cannot stand still. You wiggle all the time like one of those brown things in the ground, a—" He stopped pacing the floor and yelled, "A what do you call it?"

"A worm?" she hazarded.

"Yes, that is it. A worm!" Andrei exclaimed, making "worm" sound more like "vermin."

Leah looked up and her blue eyes narrowed. "Will you stop yelling at me!" she said in a smooth, even voice.

Andrei stopped whatever he was about to say and stared at Leah.

Leah carefully smoothed the wrinkles out of the clingy nylon skirt and stepped away from the drapery Andrei had arranged as a backdrop. "Andrei, I came here today to help you. If you don't want me to be here, I can go. I have a lot to do and—"

Andrei shook his head. "I not mean to yell. Not at all. I just want you to stand still. That is all. For only a few more minutes." He folded his hands in a prayerful gesture. "Please. I thought of all girls, you were the one who would be best standing still."

Leah sighed. Maybe it was the weather, or the fumes from the turpentine Andrei was using, but she was getting a terrible headache. "No, Andrei. I made a mistake telling you I could do this today. With the competition coming up, and nowhere to practice—I should at least be at the library studying dance tapes." Leah realized she sounded a little frantic, but that was how she felt.

Andrei picked up his brushes and put them gently back into the coffee tin. "I do not understand why you are this nervous. I am sure you can win—very easily."

Andrei's confidence failed to put Leah's mind at rest. "Well, I'm not so sure. I had a terrible practice session just now—and I—" Leah felt as if she were going to burst out crying. She took a deep breath and folded her arms across her chest. "Everything's going wrong, Andrei, everything! I can't stand it anymore." Leah pressed her fingers to her temples.

Andrei put his hand on her shoulder. "I am sorry, Leah. I see now you are under too much pressure to stand still and be my model." Andrei waited until she looked up and met his eyes. "I can finish later without you."

Leah breathed a sigh of relief. She could tell from his voice that there would be no hard feelings. "Then I can go to the library now, and maybe watching Plisetskaya one more time will help me."

Andrei shook his head. "No. That is not the way. The way is to dance the steps again and again until they become your steps—Leah's swan, not Maya's swan. Do you understand?" His hand was still on Leah's shoulder. She understood him—a little too well, she thought. She was doomed to dance just like herself. At the moment, being herself didn't seem good enough. Why couldn't she have born with technique like Finola's, or a back like Alex's, or arms like Maya Plisetskaya's?

"You go, put your clothes back on." He pointed to the bathroom door. "Then go home and go to sleep and tomorrow I will help you."

Leah grabbed her shawl and dance bag and looked up at him. "You'll help me?" she asked disbelievingly.

"Yes."

"But aren't you in the middle of rehearsals with the Company? Isn't there a performance tomorrow night at the Opera House?"

"Yes and yes." Andrei laughed, immensely pleased with himself. "But I am not in the performance tomorrow night, and the practice room downstairs are not in use during performance."

Leah hesitated. "But I don't know if I'm allowed to go there. Madame didn't say anything about—"

Andrei put his finger to her lips. "Madame cannot object if I invite you to come with me to work at the Opera House. I teach here, I coach you. I have even partnered you, no?"

Leah found herself smiling. "Yes—to all of the above. If you could help me with Odette's solo, I know I'd have a pretty good chance of winning that competition."

Andrei gave Leah a puzzled look. "You are a strange girl. I do not understand how you think you will not win. And if you do not, you will not have to leave the school. It is not the end of the world, correct?"

Leah thought to herself, she wouldn't have to leave SFBA if she didn't win. But why should she stay? Being a second-rate dancer wasn't worth all the sweat and hard work. Leah belonged on top, or she belonged nowhere in the dance world. But she couldn't tell Andrei how she felt, not now.

"I won't worry about the contest now that I have the chance to work with you," she said, smiling. She bowed graciously and clapped her hands together as if applauding Andrei at the end of a class, then hurried off to change.

When Leah returned from changing her clothes, Andrei looked lost in his painting. She tiptoed up behind him. "Good-bye, and thanks," she whispered.

"See you tomorrow," he said distractedly. "I pick you up outside the side gate after school. We practice then. Okay?"

"Yes, Andrei, and thank you so much—again."

Leah went outside feeling immensely relieved that Andrei had come to her rescue. Having Finola help her win felt wrong, but Andrei was a teacher as well as a famous dancer and accepting his help made sense. For the first time in days she felt as if her dancing was worth something again. If Andrei believed in her enough to think she could win, and to take the time to make sure she did, then maybe she had a chance to prove herself to everyone after all.

When Leah arrived back at the boardinghouse, she was cold and wet from her long walk in the rain. She hung her yellow slicker on the coatrack next to Katrina's green jacket. She was pleased to see that her friend was still at the house.

Mrs. Hanson called to Leah from the kitchen to help herself to the evening's leftovers, but Leah begged off. She had stopped at a Mexican takeout place on the way home, and her stomach still felt full from the combination of cheese enchiladas, salsa, and guacamole dip she had eaten. As her stomach grumbled, Leah cheerfully whistled the music from the solo of *Swan Lake* and bounded up the stairs two at a time.

Leah reached the small landing halfway up the first flight of stairs and rounded the corner. Katrina was on her way down. "Hi!" Leah smiled. "Your face looks better," she said warmly to Katrina.

Katrina's swollen cheek had gone down, but as

Leah looked at her more closely, she saw that Katrina had been crying. Katrina continued to stare at Leah, and her bottom lip began to tremble. The hurt in her eyes was so plain that Leah suspected something awful must have happened. "Katrina!" Leah gasped. "What's wrong? What happened?" Taking care not to brush against Leah, Katrina turned and headed down the stairs, her head held high.

Leah swung around and peered over the banister, totally baffled. "Katrina?" Leah called after her.

At the sound of her voice, Katrina yanked her jacket off the coatrack and bolted out the boardinghouse door. Leah stood on the steps, gaping at the closed door. Suddenly she knew what must have happened.

Kay had told Katrina about her plan, and how Leah was going to compete even though Katrina desperately needed the scholarship and she didn't. "Wait until I get ahold of Kay Larkin!" Leah murmured aloud. She ran the rest of the way up to the second floor.

Alex's room was at the top of the stairs, and her door was open wide. Out of habit, Leah stopped to look in. The sight that greeted Leah's eyes from just inside the door was not very inviting. Everyone who lived at the house was inside, talking. Voices hushed as Leah appeared at the door. Whoever was in Alex's room had to be talking about Leah. Leah looked around the gaily decorated room. Alex stood at the side of her bed and looked right at her.

Behind Alex, lying on her stomach amid the heap of magenta, pink, purple, and yellow cushions on the bed, was Kay. Kay treated Leah to a cold, disdainful stare. From the hall Leah could see Linda and Suzanne as well.

"Hi. What's going on?" Leah asked, stepping into the doorway.

Linda stared disapprovingly at Leah and turned away from her. Suzanne looked uncertainly from Alex to Kay then lowered her eyes. Kay and Alex traded glances. Leah frowned and put one hand against the doorframe to steady herself. Whatever she'd done, she managed to make every friend she had at SFBA mad at her. That much was obvious.

Alex finally spoke up. "I did not think you would do something like this, Leah. I thought you should compete for the scholarship, yes. But I always believed you were a fair and honest person."

"What are you talking about?" Leah asked, totally puzzled.

Kay sat up on the bed and folded her legs beneath her. "How can you still act so innocent?" she asked, her voice trembling.

"Because I have no idea what I've done. You're obviously all furious with me—and Katrina looked at me as if I'd just killed her best friend! I wish someone would let me in on the secret. You know—who, what, where, and when?"

Linda turned away in disgust.

"You didn't give Katrina her copy of the practice schedule Madame gave you this afternoon," Suzanne explained.

Leah closed her eyes and sank back against the doorframe. "Oh, no!" she wailed, annoyed at her forgetfulness. But why was everyone so upset about that? Her eyes popped open. "You mean she was slated to practice today?"

No one answered Leah. Four pairs of eyes stared at her. "I meant to give it to her here tonight," she hurried on to explain. "When I saw her at school I was on my way to pose for Andrei and I totally forgot about the schedule—I didn't think it would matter if I didn't get it to her until—" Leah looked at the accusing faces of her friends and didn't bother finishing. "You don't believe me!" she cried, horrified.

"Surely you don't *expect* us to," Kay retorted. She ran her fingers through her short-cropped curls and glared at Leah. Then she jumped off the bed and strode over to the door. She looked up at Leah and rested her hands on her tiny hips. "I thought you were the one person around this place that a girl could trust. But I should have known that when you wouldn't back down from the competition, all you really care about is yourself, numero uno, the Great Stephenson!"

"That's not fair, Kay!" Leah's confusion was quickly giving way to anger. "I have every right to compete! If Katrina is going to hate me for it, she might as well hate Linda, or Pam, or a dozen other girls who refused to take their names off the list."

"This has nothing to do with competing on Wednesday," Alex pointed out. "Leah's right. Competing for the Adams is all right for her to do." Kay began to protest, but Alex put up her hand.

With barely veiled sarcasm Leah bowed her head. "How kind of you to give me permission to compete!"

Alex return her icy stare.

"Leah, it's not a matter of competing or not," Linda said next. "It's a matter of sabotaging Katrina. Now she has only one half hour to practice before the competition. A half hour! Madame had purposely given her practice time late this afternoon so she could squeeze it in after the dentist and before dinner. But she missed it because of you. How would you feel if you were in her shoes?"

Leah couldn't answer that, at least not right away. She looked away from Linda's questioning eyes and studied the pattern of the woven straw throw rug at the foot of Alex's bed. After a few tense moments of silence she admitted. "I'd be very upset. I might even be angry. But I'd understand it was a reasonable mistake!" Leah's voice rose slightly on the last couple of words.

Kay rolled her eyes. "It's too convenient a mistake, Leah. For some reason you don't want Katrina to win this competition. I don't care what Alex or anyone else says, the fact that you're in it pretty much ruins Katrina's chances. And conveniently forgetting to give Katrina her schedule is really the last straw. She doesn't have a chance now! Someone should go to Madame and tell her what you've done to Katrina," Kay practically yelled.

"Girls, what is going on up there?" Mrs. Hanson's concerned voice floated up the stairwell.

"Nothing, Mrs. Hanson," Leah and Alex answered at the same time.

"Just a discussion," Leah added. She lowered her voice and her tone was cool and very even. "Kay, I've been thinking of doing the exact same thing! If I went to Madame and told her you rigged this competition so Katrina would win by default, you'd be in big trouble!"

"Stop it—both of you!" Alex commanded. Her almond-shaped eyes flashed with anger, and two red spots burned on her cheeks. "No one is going to Madame about anything. If Leah wants to play dirty tricks, that is her business. No one has gone to Madame about Pam, for instance, in the past, and I do not think it is right to start going to her now." She looked hard at Kay, who lowered her eyes and sat down with a resigned sigh on the edge of Alex's bed. "I do not know if you are telling the truth, Leah," Alex began slowly. "Even if you think you forgot about the schedule by accident, I have a feeling you would do almost anything to win this competition." She paused as if to give Leah a chance to reveal exactly why she was so determined to win the scholarship. "Maybe you forgot accidentally on purpose."

"Accident or no accident," Linda commented in an acid voice. "Katrina's chances were poor before. Without practice she might as well forget about entering."

But Leah couldn't accept that. "Whatever happens to Katrina on Wednesday, you can't blame me for everything," she cried. "And for what it's worth, I'm glad I'm not Katrina. I'd hate to think my so-called friends had so little faith in the possibility of my winning that they had to get rid of all the other competitors!" With that Leah turned on her heel and ran up the stairs to her room on the third floor. She slammed the door hard and the whole house seemed to shake.

Leah stood in the middle of her room, trying to catch her breath. Her heart was beating so fast she wondered if she was going to faint. Misha, her kitten, jumped down from the windowsill and walked toward her. He arched his back and rubbed against her leg. The feel of his warm, furry body seemed to break down all Leah's reserve. She bent over and picked up the little cat. She held Misha closer in her arms and started to cry.

"How—how could—they believe that, Misha?" she moaned. "How could they? I wouldn't do that to my worst enemy. How could they think I would try to hurt Katrina?"

Leah lay down carefully on her bed and held Misha tightly. "At least you," she gasped between sobs, "you're still my friend!"

Chapter 9

Leah had never been to a high school
dance, but now she knew exactly what it meant
to be a wallflower.

Tuesday afternoon's character class was one of
the highlights of the week for SFBA students. The
atmosphere was less formal than in other classes.
The girls wore dirndl skirts over their leotards
and sometimes dance slippers with low heels.
The national and folk dances the boys and girls
learned were often difficult, but learning them
was somehow more fun than enduring the rigors
of the school's classical ballet classes, or the
Graham technique modern dance session. Leah
excelled at character dances; she had the ability
to easily mimic different ethnic dance styles. And,
of course, being the girl all the boys wanted to
dance with made the class even more enjoyable
for Leah.

Today not one boy wanted to dance with Leah.
She stood alone near the barre, her cheeks burning as Patrick Hogan finished giving instructions
to Robert, the accompanist. When the sandy-haired
teacher turned around and saw Leah standing

without a partner, Patrick ran his fingers through his thinning hair and frowned. Usually Patrick was left to partner Pam. Leah could almost read his mind as he looked around the room and finally spotted Pam standing next to Daniel Archot, a new boy from France, who didn't exactly look very happy with his chosen partner.

Leah continued to stare straight ahead of her. She tried to ignore the fact that Michael Litvak was just four steps away talking animatedly to Finola. Leah wasn't sure what hurt more, the fact that Michael had chosen Finola out of all the other girls in the room, or the fact that Finola was avoiding her today. Katrina and Kay had obviously spread the news. Not one student Leah knew seemed to be talking to her. No one so much as looked her way in morning class; she had sat at a table all by herself in the crowded lunchroom at noon, and not one person had tried to join her. Now she was being blatantly ostracized by the boys and the girls in the class. Leah wanted to turn around and scream and tell everyone they were being unfair. She had never meant to hurt Katrina, to blow her chances at winning the scholarship! But apparently Kay had already convinced everyone that Leah Stephenson wasn't the sweet, blond angel she seemed to be but, instead, a nasty little witch.

Leah looked up when Patrick arrived at her side. "I see I'm the lucky one today," he said quietly. Leah squeezed the hand he offered her, feeling extremely grateful. Whatever the other students had against Leah didn't matter to Patrick.

With as much poise and dignity as if she were taking her place center stage, Leah walked with her hand lightly on Patrick's arm to the middle of the studio floor, conscious that the whole room was watching her, having prejudged her as a girl who would step over everyone—even poor Katrina—to get what she wanted. As he turned around to face the other students, Patrick continued to hold her hand. Leah kept her eyes focused right in front of her, glad there weren't mirrors up by the piano so she didn't have to watch the other kids watch her.

"We started studying the mazurka last week, remember?" Patrick asked the class. "It's a very emotional dance with great spirit as well. The feeling is all in the top of the body." Patrick turned to Alex. "You're an old hand at mazurkas, Alex. Would you demonstrate the first few steps of the one we were learning?" Patrick signaled Robert to start, and Leah knew she had no choice but to turn around and watch.

With a proud tilt of her chin, and deliberately avoiding Leah's eyes, Alex waited for the first four bars of Robert's music. Then she sprang into action. The high arch of her back, the angle of her head, and the fire in her eyes were truly inspirational. She clicked her heels together strongly and her whole body seemed to smolder with a barely restrained passion. Leah watched with a curious mix of emotions. The dancer in her drank in every nuance of Alex's style: her gestures, the exact position of her arms, the tricks she had of brushing her skirt with her hand or casting her eyes toward the imagined audience for a particular effect. But the girl in Leah was on the verge of tears: Until yesterday Alex had been her best friend at SFBA. Now even Alex didn't believe in her anymore. Alex thought of her as a low, two-faced person who was no better than Pam.

After ten bars of the mazurka, Patrick lifted his hand and told Alex to stop. He gave her an approving look, then smiled at the class. "Of course Alex has some Eastern European fire in her blood, and she has been studying national dances since she was a small girl in Leningrad. But by watching her, you can learn a lot. Let's try to break the movements down a little as we move on to the section where you work with a partner." He turned to Leah and gave her an encouraging smile. Leah couldn't manage to smile back. Patrick's eyebrows arched slightly, but he took Leah's hand firmly. While he demonstrated the next combination of steps he kept talking, his voice raised so the roomful of students behind him could hear his detailed instructions.

Leah listened to the sound of shuffles, steps, little jumps, and clicking heels. She tried to keep up with Patrick, but for once her knack for catching on to new combinations of steps seemed to desert her. Finally Patrick dropped her hand and reproved her with a look. "Are you feeling all right?" he asked loudly enough for everyone in the room to hear.

Behind Leah, Kay cleared her throat. A low buzz of voices went around the room. Patrick turned to the other students and frowned. Immediately the room fell silent. "Let's try it again," he announced. "This time with music. I think *everyone* here was having problems with that combination." Patrick took Leah's hand again and with his other hand motioned for Robert to start playing. Patrick counted four bars aloud, but when he moved to the front on the fifth bar of the music, Leah found her feet rooted to the spot.

All Leah could think was that she couldn't take

it anymore. Everyone was being so unfair and mean to her. She didn't deserve being treated so poorly, no matter what.

Patrick stopped dancing and Robert's music died off. Leah dropped Patrick's hand, turned on her heel, and forced herself to walk slowly to the door. She knew she should have asked permission to leave, but she was afraid if she opened her mouth, she might say something awful. The other students stepped aside and made room for her to walk out. Leah picked up her towel and her dance bag and proceeded straight into the hallway without bothering to go into the changing room.

As soon as the squeaky door to the Blue Studio shut tightly behind her, Leah quickened her pace. By the time she got to the bathroom she was running. She pushed open the door. Sun streamed through the window and the clean white tiles gleamed. The brilliant light was almost too bright for Leah's mood. She leaned back against the sink nearest the window and hugged her arms around her chest. Her bottom lip began to tremble. Last night, with Misha in her arms, Leah had cried herself to sleep. She had wept so long and hard, she had been sure she would have no tears left this morning. But now her eyes were full again. And first one tear and then another ran down her face and dropped onto her bare arms. Leah felt as if she could cry forever. She leaned her head against the cool tiles of the windowsill and sobbed loudly in the empty room.

After a long time her tears subsided, and thoughts started to fill her head. What had she done to deserve all this? For a moment she thought of going to Madame and pouring her heart out.

But doing that would be betraying a friend: Kay would be sure to get into trouble, and Katrina's dilemma was something Madame would have to learn about from Katrina herself. It wasn't really Leah's business. She rubbed the tears from her cheek with the back of her hand then turned the cold water on in the sink.

Leah splashed cold water on her face again and again. Her head was pounding. Leah couldn't remember ever having cried quite as much as this. Then the memory came back to her: The last time had been after her father had died. She had been only nine years old. She hadn't cried at the funeral. All day long at school and after school at Miss Greene's dance class she hadn't shed a tear. But at night, alone in her bed, Leah would start to cry and not be able to stop, not even when her mother came into her room and tried to comfort her. That was a long time ago now. Leah had never thought she would feel that hollow and empty and lost inside again.

She was still bent over the sink when someone came into the room. Whoever it was, she had stopped at the door. She waited a moment, then cleared her throat. Finally Leah looked up.

"I thought you'd left," Katrina said, her voice flat, emotionless.

Leah's first instinct was to pretend Katrina just wasn't there and leave the room, but she reached for a paper towel to dry her face. Then she turned around and faced Katrina. She forced herself not to shrink back from the accusing look in Katrina's soulful eyes.

"Katrina, I'm sorry about your schedule. I know what you—what everybody thinks. It's not true. I really forgot to give it to you." Leah's voice was hoarse from crying, but she didn't flinch from Katrina's steady gaze.

Katrina stuffed her fists into the pockets of her jean jacket and stared at Leah. "There's nothing to be sorry about. What's done is done." Katrina continued in a quiet voice, "I'm only sorry that I was wrong about you. I thought you were the one girl in the school I could trust. That's why I told you about my parents before I told anyone else."

Katrina walked over to the sink and reached for a paper towel. She moistened it under the cold water and dabbed at a spot on her jacket. She gave a careless little shrug. "I actually looked up to you, Leah Stephenson."

"You shouldn't have done that," Leah said quickly. "I don't want to be looked up to. I want to be your friend and I want people to believe me."

Katrina gripped the edge of the sink tightly with her thin hands. "No one will ever believe you again, not after this. I don't mind that you're trying for the same scholarship. But to turn out to be a two-faced liar like Pam Hunter—"

Katrina shook her head. "You know it makes me wonder if being a dancer is worth any of this. I almost hope I lose tomorrow. That way I can go home and forget all about my dreams. I'm beginning to think the world of dance is really a nightmare."

Katrina lifted her bag onto her shoulder and slammed the door on her way out.

"And what do you think *you're* doing here?" Diana's voice was hostile enough to make Leah wonder if she had been privy to the latest round of Academy gossip.

Andrei put down his dance bag and gave Diana a puzzled look. He and Leah were in the hallway leading to the Opera House rehearsal studios. They were standing right beneath the orchestra pit, and Leah could hear an oboe practicing a series of runs from a ballet score she couldn't quite place.

"I invited Leah here to work with me." Andrei's answer was simple, direct, and didn't give away much.

"I suppose she talked you into giving her extra coaching sessions for that competition tomorrow," Diana said.

Leah's nerves were frayed enough; this time she had to speak up for herself. "Andrei offered to help me. Was I supposed to turn him down?"

Diana's artfully tweezed eyebrows arched significantly. She smoothed the arms of the long blue puffy-sleeved costume she was wearing.

Leah suddenly recognized the score: It was from the first act of *Romeo and Juliet.* Leah had forgotten all about that evening's big performance. It was the season premier of the Prokofiev ballet, and Patrick and Diana were dancing the leads. Leah wondered if Diana had noticed the tiny speck of pink paint on the hem of her dress for the last act.

"It's not up to me to say what you can or can't do," Diana said in a tone that contradicted her words. "It just doesn't seem fair to the other girls competing..." Diana's voice trailed off and she fixed her dark eyes on Leah.

"I think it is fair for any dancer to get all the help she can," Andrei asserted.

Again Diana shrugged. "Well, I'm not a judge!" To Leah she said, "Break a leg—tomorrow that is.

Frankly, I think you'd make the best swan of everyone who signed up. I hope you get it." With that Diana allowed herself to be pecked on the cheek by Andrei, then she vanished up the side stairs.

Leah gaped at Diana as she disappeared and shook her head. "Every time I think that woman hates me, she suddenly says something nice," Leah explained.

"She does not hate you. You frighten her. That is all."

"That's what Alex—" Leah cut herself off and bit her lip. She didn't want to talk about Alex now, or Finola, or anyone else. "Let's get to work," she said in a businesslike tone. Together she and Andrei marched down the dimly lit hall toward the practice rooms.

Andrei flicked on the studio lights and strode over to the electrical outlet to plug in the tape player. Leah pulled off her street clothes. She was still wearing her tights and leotard from character class that afternoon. While Andrei fast-forwarded the cassette to find the exact spot of Odette's solo, Leah put on her toe shoes. She tied the ribbons very carefully and tried to clear her mind of everything but the choreography she intended to practice.

She almost had herself fooled at first. Andrei listened to the music, marked out the steps both for his sake and hers, then asked her to mark her way through it once, giving her suggestions for interpretation. Then the time came to dance it full out. Leah gritted her teeth, determined not to repeat yesterday's disastrous performance.

But halfway through the solo Andrei jumped up. "Stop. Stop!" he cried. He shut off the tape recorder and glared at Leah. "What is the matter with you? I see you dance in class, onstage. I even dance with you. You never look so—so—" He fished for the word.

Leah had no idea what Andrei was getting at. She had felt strong dancing, as if her feet had finally mastered the steps.

Andrei threw his hands in the air. "You do not look like a graceful big white swan. You look like a terrible bird. A—I think it is named a crow!"

Leah stepped back, horrified.

"You don't make your arms like this, and your legs like this." Andrei pranced around the room, every movement of his supple body jerky and ugly.

"I didn't dance like that!" Leah protested.

"No," Andrei said. "You danced worse." He paced to the corner of the small studio, pounded his fist on the old upright piano, and paced back again. He bent down toward Leah. "You must not dance like this. It is as if you want to kill somebody with every step. As if you make your feet like little knives, and the floor is someone's heart. You dance like that," he said with absolute conviction, "you hurt yourself so bad you never dance again."

Leah believed Andrei, but she didn't want to hear anymore. She stomped to the corner and grabbed her sweater and started stuffing her overalls, her leg warmers, and her pink sneakers back into her dance bag. As she packed her things, she complained bitterly, "I didn't ask you to help me. If you want to make fun of my dancing and tell me I look like a crow, that's your business. I can't stop you from thinking what you want about me. But I don't have to stand here listening to you." Leah straightened up and glared at Andrei. Her eyes were dark with anger, but she felt a familiar catch in the back of her throat. She would not, she *must* not, cry now.

Andrei stared at her, a series of expressions flickering across his face. He looked angry, surprised, and sympathetic all at once. "Leah, what is making you like this? You are not yourself."

His voice was so gentle Leah almost gave in to her tears. She wanted someone to hold her, to listen to her side of the story, to tell her that she hadn't hurt Katrina, that she wasn't wrong to fear Finola, that desperately wanting to win the Adams Scholarship wasn't a terrible thing.

Andrei walked over to Leah. "I ask you on Sunday to talk to me, to tell me what is the matter. You were not ready then. You were not ready yesterday. You say it is the competition. But I think it is more than that."

Leah turned her face away from his. She grabbed the barre and held on to it tightly until the knuckles of her hands turned white. "Everything's wrong, Andrei. Just everything," she whispered to the wall.

Leah was glad Andrei didn't try to comfort her then or touch her or hug her. He just stood behind her, kept still, and waited for her to speak. At first she kept her back to him and poured it all out: How everything began when she saw Finola dance, how suddenly nothing was more important to her than winning the scholarship, how Katrina's problem with money and tuition didn't matter to Leah, how all that mattered was winning. When she finally turned to face him, tears were streaming down her cheeks and her waterproof mascara had failed her once again.

"This is not such a terrible thing," Andrei told her.

"Today Katrina said I was exactly like Pam," Leah confided.

"You are not at all like that girl Pam!" Andrei bellowed across the empty studio. "She is a very sad girl. I pity her."

Leah was so shocked that she stared right at Andrei and stopped crying.

"You are happy," Andrei explained. "You dance from here." He thumped his heart with his hand. "That is your gift. You are the perfect size for a prima ballerina. You are lyrical. You have very good technique. I have seen better. Pam has better. Maybe Finola does, but I have not seen her dance. But you have this gift very few people have. Pam does not have it at all. Sometimes when I watch her I feel she is the way you were just now, full of hate. I feel she hates to dance. She treats every step like a battle in a war. No, you are not like Pam."

Leah sank back against the barre. "I don't understand you, Andrei," she said, and looked up at him with wondering eyes. "You don't know Pam at all, and yet what you say about her is more right than anything I've ever thought of before. I just thought she was competitive and mean-spirited."

"She is that, too. And I do not say she is not gifted in her way as a dancer. Her anger makes for great strength. But she will never be half the artist you already are."

"But Pam isn't the problem, Andrei," Leah said after a moment's thought. "The real problem is Finola. I know that she's already twice the artist I'll ever be." The words she had been so afraid to say out loud came easily to Leah now.

The hope that Andrei would say Finola couldn't

possibly be better than Leah was dashed quickly. "Maybe she is. I hear from Madame, from everyone, she is remarkable," Andrei said. "I notice her in the halls. She has a grace when she walks. She is special. But you are special, too. So is Alex, and Kay, and so many other girls here. Many different kinds of dancers have become great."

Leah listened carefully to Andrei's words. She shrugged on her cardigan and looked up at him, a little embarrassed but happy that her torrent of tears was over. Nothing had been solved by this conversation with Andrei, yet Leah felt better, as if a terrible burden had been lifted from her shoulders.

"I think maybe we need to talk more, but no more dancing tonight. You should go home and rest. However"—Andrei flashed his famous grin—"we have dinner first. Chinatown maybe?"

Leah patted her stomach. She let out a surprised laugh. "I am hungry. I haven't really eaten in ages—or at least not since last night," she corrected herself.

"You go take shower in dressing room. Take your time. Fix your makeup and your hair. We will pretend this is a date!"

Leah laughed. It was good having Andrei as a friend. "I have to call Mrs. Hanson—"

"I call her for you," Andrei interrupted quickly. "I have call to make, too."

When Leah came out of the dressing room, both Alex and Andrei were waiting for her. The distant music of the balcony scene filled the air. Leah stood very still and met Alex's gaze. Neither girl spoke.

"I ask Alex to join us for dinner," Andrei said. "I

think you need a friend—a friend who is a girl your age and who is not an old teacher."

Alex surprised Leah with her warm smile. "Andrei talked to me. He explained everything." Tears shone in Alex's eyes as she threw open her arms. The next minute Leah was hugging Alex, tears running down her own face and for the third time that day ruining her makeup.

Finally Alex stepped back and held Leah at arm's length. "Why did you not talk to me sooner? Why did you not tell me about Finola?"

Alex led Leah to a narrow bench, and the two girls sat down, resting their backs against the cool concrete wall. Andrei leaned against the closed door of one of the dressing rooms and worked his right ankle around in circles while the girls started to talk.

"I thought you wouldn't understand," Leah admitted in a small voice. Then she frowned. She looked directly at Alex and said a little stiffly, "I wasn't so wrong, was I? You didn't believe me, about how that forgotten schedule was all a big mistake."

"Touché!" Alex said quietly. But she lifted a warning finger as Leah began to smile. "It was a mistake. I see that now. You did not mean to forget to give her her schedule. And you did not know—consciously—that if she got it a day late, it would hurt her performance tommorrow. I see that. But you must see that sometimes if you want something very much, like winning a competition, your mind will play tricks on you. It will make you forget something."

Leah allowed Alex's words to sink in. She looked up, frightened. "That's scary. If Katrina loses tomorrow because of me—and I don't mean because of my dancing—then I don't know how I'll live with it."

Andrei leaned down in front of the girls and took Leah's hand between his. He massaged it gently. "It is not such a terrible thing to want to win."

Leah pulled back. "Not even if you want to win for terrible reasons?"

"Nothing's so terrible about wanting to be a better dancer than Finola," Alex commented. "When you came here, and I saw you the first time in Madame's class, I hated you, too."

"Alexandra Sorokin!" Leah gasped.

"I did. Before you came here I was the best dancer Madame had taught in years. The minute I saw you at the barre that day, when Diana taught the first class, I knew I would no longer be Madame's star pupil."

Andrei nodded sagely. "I had that happen to me, too."

Both Alex and Leah looked at Andrei, surprised. At nineteen he was already what some critics called the greatest male dancer of his generation.

"I was at the Vaganova Institute, it was my last year. I was about sixteen or seventeen and already they had a place for me in the company. Then this fifteen-year-old boy comes along, with very little classical training. He looks and moves exactly like Nureyev. No one talked about my elevation for two years after that."

Andrei looked so despondent at the memory that both girls started to laugh.

Alex turned to Leah again. "You just have to get used to there being more than one star in the sky."

At Alex's words Leah took a deep breath. "That's

a beautiful way of putting it." Leah smiled to herself for a moment. Then her face grew very serious. "But I have to talk to Katrina first thing tomorrow. I have to tell her how sorry I am and how I understand now what happened."

Suddenly Andrei leapt to his feet from his crouching position in front of Leah. "The balcony scene is almost over, and this hallway will have a lot of people in it soon. We should get out of here." He put his hand on his stomach and pretended to stagger down the hall. "I am dying if I do not eat soon!"

"Then onward and upward," Alex said with a flourish. "To Chinatown."

She hooked Leah's hand through her right arm and Andrei's through her left, and pulled them down the hall.

"To Chinatown!" Leah echoed, and with a light heart she went out the stage door, laughing with her friends.

Chapter 10

"This place is the pits!" Pamela Hunter cried in dismay the next afternoon. Leah, Pam, and several second-year SFBA students stood outside a ramshackle movie theater on the outskirts of a slightly rundown neighborhood Leah had never seen before. The marquee sported a rim of new light fixtures and straight black letters that spelled *La Casa De Bernarda Alba.* Leah's Spanish was pretty minimal, but she figured the title of the play had to be something like "Bernarda Alba's House." Raul had told Leah that his Teatro Hispánico was doing a classic of the modern Spanish stage this month. Raul was parking the van in the Teatro's lot around the corner.

The small group of SFBA students waiting on the sidewalk was the last of the Adams Scholarship contestants to be chauffeured from the school. Leah had been glad the luck of the draw hadn't landed her in the same vanload as Katrina or Linda or any of the other girls who had been giving her the cold shoulder. The previous night's resolve to talk to Katrina was still uppermost in Leah's mind, but so far she hadn't had a chance.

"It's certainly a dreary setting for an audition," Lindsay Kohlmeier remarked, screwing her face up in a frown.

Leah could understand the other girls' reactions to the one place Madame was able to find at that last minute to hold the Adams competition. But Raul had always referred to it as his place, and that made it good enough for Leah.

Raul rounded the corner and led the girls to a door just behind the box office. Just inside, Sandy Waldbaum, one of the apprentices with the Company, was sitting on a tall metal stool. She had a clipboard in her hand and a pencil tucked above her ear. Sandy's face was pleasant and she greeted the nervous contestants with a sympathetic smile. Leah waited nervously while she ran through the names: "Hunter, Kohlmeier, Picchi—" Sandy looked up and pointed to the left of the lobby. "You three go down to the dressing room on that side of the stage. Most of the girls who arrived earlier are there." She read Leah's name next, along with the four second-year students next to her. "The rest of you go to the right and down that hall. You'll find mirrors and some makeup. If you need anything, some actresses from Raul's company who volunteered to help will be happy to give you a hand. The contest will begin in twenty minutes. Be warmed up and onstage by then."

Leah was the first of her group into the dressing room. She set her bag down on the chair farthest from the door, relieved that she didn't have to get dressed and make small talk with people who knew her well. She pulled out a clean towel, folded it, and laid it on top of the small makeup area. Then she unpacked her toe shoes, some extra elastics for her hair, a can of hair spray, and a fine, pale brown net to keep every wisp of hair in her bun in place during allegro work and pirouettes. She pulled a small makeup case out of her bag and unzipped it. Inside were mascara, dark eyeliner, and a special assortment of dramatically colored eye shadows and blushes that would accentuate her features under the bright lights onstage.

Since coming to SFBA Leah had developed her own special ritual that she performed before beginning to dress for any audition or performance. And no matter how crazy she was feeling inside, she kept to her routine. It steadied her somehow.

After her things were laid out in the proper order, Leah looked in the mirror. She jumped a little when she saw Linda regarding her quietly from the opposite corner of the room. She hadn't expected to see Linda. She thought the girls who had arrived earlier had all been assigned to the other dressing room. She looked past Linda's reflection half expecting to see Kay, but Kay wasn't there.

Linda surprised Leah by smiling, and then she began to walk over. Leah turned around slowly and got ready to defend her actions with Katrina.

"I'm sorry, Leah. Alex explained everything to me after class this morning, and to Kay, too," Linda said.

Leah sighed with relief. "Thanks, Linda. I guess it was all just a misunderstanding." Leah didn't know what else to say, but Linda rescued her with another friendly smile.

"It happens between the best of friends. And now we've all got to go out there and wow those judges!" Linda exclaimed.

Leah laughed nervously. For a moment she had

been so worried about her problems with the other girls, she had forgotten all about the competition. As they changed their clothes and touched up their makeup, Leah and Linda ended up making small talk after all with the rest of the girls. They discussed that morning's class and how great it would feel when things at the school were back to normal and Madame could resume teaching their daily class.

Supporting herself on the back of a chair, Linda began her warm-ups. Leah excused herself and left the room. There was one piece of business that had to be finished before the contest started. Leah made her way across the unfamiliar backstage area toward the other dressing room. Halfway there, she stopped. Katrina had her right leg propped up on a horizontal pipe that looked like it was connected to the theater's heating system. The brown-haired girl's well-pointed foot was actually trembling as she bent her torso forward and let her forehead come to rest on the knee of the upraised leg.

Katrina's body language quickly told Leah that she was very nervous and still quite upset. Leah's resolve to clear the air before they both had to get onstage and go through with the audition wavered. She didn't want to risk upsetting Katrina even more.

Just then Karina looked up. Her large brown eyes had a frightened and hurt expression, and her lips were pursed together tightly, as if she were trying to hold something in. She didn't look angry anymore. She lifted her leg off the makeshift barre, pulled up her leg warmers, and marched up to Leah.

"Alex told me after class today what happened when—"

Leah held up her hand to stop Katrina. It was one thing for Alex to explain the situation to Linda or any other girl who hadn't been affected by Leah's actions, but Leah had to tell Katrina the whole story herself. "What Alex said isn't the point," Leah insisted in a low, steady voice. She glanced around. Anything at all in the backstage area that could be used as a barre was occupied, and Leah didn't want anyone to overhear her. She pulled Katrina behind a gloomy-looking set: It had a huge full moon painted above what looked to be a ghost town of crooked gray stone houses.

"But it was a mistake, Leah, I see that now," Katrina said once they were in private.

"It was and it wasn't." Leah smoothed back her hair. She looked right into Katrina's eyes. She had to make her understand somehow. "I did forget. But maybe, down deep inside I wanted to win so badly that I would do anything to come out first. So I forgot because it was convenient. I didn't know that at the time. But sometimes you do things without knowing why."

Katrina took a deep breath. "But wanting to win is all right, Leah. Even wanting to win that bad." She looked around quickly then beckoned Leah to come even closer. "You are not like Pam," she whispered. "I never should have said that. You're not two-faced. You didn't plan to sabotage me. Pam plots, you don't."

The two girls traded shy smiles then hugged each other. When she pulled away, Leah was dismayed to see Katrina still looking sad. "I hope you do well today," Leah said, pressing her hand and hoping to cheer her.

Katrina let out a tired little laugh. "Well, at least you thought enough of my dancing to worry that I might win. At least you thought I was competition."

Leah regarded Katrina with a puzzled tilt of her head.

"I found out about Kay and her great plan," Katrina said bitterly.

Leah's mouth formed a silent Oh!

"Finola told me this morning. She was very angry. She yelled at Kay." Katrina brightened at the memory, then her face fell. "But I have never felt so humiliated in all my life. I need this scholarship. I need to win. But I couldn't possibly accept that money if I thought the competition was fixed!"

"Yeah, Alex said you would feel like that." Leah had said that, too, but she had said it only to cover up her own motives for staying in the competition.

"I feel like going to Madame, but Finola made me promise I wouldn't. She said it would cause a lot of trouble for every girl who went along with Kay." Katrina looked up at Leah. "I guess she's right," she concluded uncertainly.

"She's right," Leah said, convinced of it. She felt a little embarrassed talking about Kay's plan. Leah hadn't stayed in the competition and fought so hard because she thought Katrina would win. It had never occurred to her. She tried to think of a way to change the subject. "Last night Andrei said something very important. He said that every girl here was talented. That every girl here would make a good swan. That means you, too." Leah wasn't sure those were Andrei's exact words, but she knew that was what he had meant.

Katrina looked up. "He thinks I have a chance?" She sounded amazed.

"You do have a chance," Leah said. She looked at Katrina as if truly seeing her for the first time. Katrina was delicate and pale, with a dramatic flair that suited her perfectly for something like *Giselle* or *Juliet.* But she could be a swan, too, a different sort of swan. She could be an enchanted, frail girl who needed the protection of her prince to overcome the terrible power of Van Rothbart, the sorcerer. Her fragile beauty would make the White Acts of the ballet poignant. Leah could see Katrina in a feathery white tutu, like a piece of moonlight floating over a lake. As for the bravura dancing of the third, Black Act, Leah suddenly remembered something. "You know, Katrina, some ballerinas never do the fouettés at all," Leah said encouragingly. "They do piqué turns in a circle around the stage."

Katrina's eyes lit up. "They do!" She clapped her thin hands together. "I remember that. Sometimes even two different dancers play the roles of Odette and Odile. Maybe you could be Odile and I could be Odette. Maybe we can both win somehow. Half a scholarship would keep me here one more year, and then—" Katrina laughed. "By then my parents might have gotten on their feet again—or I can try next year for the next Adams competition!"

Leah frowned. She had wanted to get Katrina's hopes up but not that high. "I don't know if Madame would go for that Odette/Odile bit," Leah said carefully.

Katrina shrugged. "Let's make a deal. If you win, then ask her. If I win—I'll ask her, too."

Katrina bit her lip and looked down. "If Pam or one of the other girls wins, well—"

"They won't! We won't give them a chance," Leah said immediately. She grabbed Katrina's hands and grinned. She wasn't going to let Katrina's spirits sag now, just moments before the competition. She owed her at least that much. "And about that deal—I'm all for it. So let's both go out there and—"

"Break a leg!" Katrina finished for her just as their names were called to join the other girls onstage.

"You call this an audition?" Pamela Hunter complained under her breath to Leah. Both girls were standing in the wings trying to catch their breath.

Leah wasn't sure what she would call it, but she wasn't about to agree with Pam. "It's not an audition. It's a competition." She took two or three steps away from the redhead and pulled her towel off the top of a prop. She mopped the sweat off her face just before her name was called again—along with Pam's, Lindsay's, Linda's, and Barbara's.

Leah tugged down the back of her damp leotard and walked on to the stage, conscious that the judges were watching her every move.

"Line up, please. Three in the front, two in the back." Madame directed the girls in a curt, businesslike voice. Leah was glad Madame was on the panel of judges—and that she had not seen Finola Darling dance as of yet.

Leah took her place at one end of the front line, Pam at the other. Behind her, Leah heard Barbara whisper a quick prayer. It was this group's third and last time onstage. Katrina's group hadn't even begun their audition yet.

Leah forced herself not to cross her fingers. So far everything had been going her way. The judges hadn't asked for anything outrageously difficult. In fact, Leah couldn't quite figure out how they were going to pick one girl when every girl onstage seemed equally good at all the steps. Leah could actually understand Pam's annoyance with the whole process. So far today's contest hadn't given Pam the chance to really strut her stuff, since the combinations Madame shouted out were not very athletic.

This time Madame selected a long adagio sequence for them. Pam groaned: Adagio was not her strength. Leah loved the slow, graceful unfoldings of the arms and legs, though she knew taller dancers like Finola or Alex always looked more beautiful performing adagio work. Their long legs and high arabesques suited the slow movements perfectly.

The next group of steps took Leah by surprise. They were taken directly from the entrance of the corps of swans in the second act of *Swan Lake.* The girls were sent back into the wings, then entered one at a time when the piano started. Pam was the first girl. Madame counted the first few bars then clapped her hands, and Pam entered stage right with what was supposed to be a small jeté with one leg in a low arabesque, followed by several prancing steps with the legs kicking out to the front. To show off her elevation, Pam jumped very high, too high, in fact, and she landed out of step with the music. By the time she reached the far end of the stage Pam was completely out of sync. Madame didn't say a thing.

The music continued and Leah was next. She

loved the particular sequence of steps and threw
herself into the dancing, pretending she was one
of Odette's handmaidens about to change from a
swan back into a girl. She sailed lightly through
the air and skimmed the surface of the floorboards, remembering to keep her feet well pointed
and her arms soft and birdlike.

When she exited through the far wing, Leah
heard one of the judges say something that
sounded like "wonderful" or "beautiful." Leah
beamed.

Within seconds Leah's group had finished.
Linda stomped around backstage growling at everyone and nothing in particular. She had started
on the wrong foot and she knew that was just
enough to put her out of the running. "Well, I
tried," she finally said, then grinned at Leah. "You
looked great. Maybe you'll get it."

Leah just shrugged, but her heart was singing.
She had performed better than anyone in her
group. Now it was Katrina's turn. She and Linda
watched from one of the wings. Madame ran
through the same combinations. The first two
sets of steps were easy, and Leah couldn't for the
life of her pick who had danced them best. When
the adagio came she was shocked to see Katrina
didn't wobble on her supporting leg for once—not
during the entire long combination.

"Pretty good!" Linda murmured in Leah's ear.

"She's getting stronger every day!" Barbara noted.

Katrina was at the end of the line when the
second group of girls danced their way through
the corps work for the swans. From her vantage
point in the wing opposite, Leah saw Katrina's
face as she struggled to remember which foot to
start on. But somehow she managed to emerge

from the wings flying through the air in the right position. Like Leah, Katrina was naturally musical. Her light jump and quick feet made her seem very much like a bird in flight as she sped through the combination.

"Great!" Linda opened her arms to help Katrina land as she jetéd into the wings.

"Terrific, Katrina!" Leah congratuled her warmly.

Linda began to spin Katrina around. "I think you did it! I think you really did it."

Sandy walked across the stage, her sneakers squeaking against the sticky rosined surface. She poked her head into the wings. "Madame says go get dressed then come down and sit in the audience. We'll announce the winner in fifteen minutes."

Leah hurried back to her dressing room, trying not to look at Linda, who was still waxing eloquent about Katrina's performance. "I'd give anything to fly through the air like that!" Linda sighed.

Not bothering to take off her stage makeup, Leah pulled her skirt over her head and grabbed the rest of her things. She dressed quickly. Leah was so nervous that she was back in the auditorium ten minutes early.

The time seemed to crawl, and Leah tried not to stare at the judges as they conferred at a long table that had been set up on the stage. Madame was there, along with Christopher Robson, a guest teacher who had been one of the judges at Leah's entrance audition to the school. A petite dancer whose upswept dark hair was streaked with gray was also there. Her features were familiar and Leah had a feeling she had once danced for George Balanchine at the New York City Ballet. Patrick Hogan was there as well.

Other girls slowly filed into the fourth row, where Leah was sitting. Pam sat down next to her and instantly began drumming her fingers against the wooden armrest. Leah looked away and saw Katrina smiling at her from the aisle seat. Leah smiled back. She remembered her promise to Katrina. If either girl won, they would approach Madame about dividing the roles of Odile and Odette.

Madame finally stood up. She shielded her eyes from the stage lights and seemed to count the girls present in the auditorium. Satisfied that everyone was there, she prefaced her remarks with a smile and a round of applause. "A very good job—considering. We tried to take into consideration the condition of the stage, the fact it had never been used for ballet before, and the fact that none of you has ever been in this theater in your lives. It is hard enough for professional dancers to audition in strange places—but it is also a fact of a dancer's life. So consider this week's problems with studio space and rehearsal time part of your training."

An audible groan went up from the girls. Madame laughed then raised her hand to silence them. "We have come to our decision. Let me say that we did discuss the idea of two girls sharing the scholarship. The dual role of Odette/Odile in *Swan Lake* lends itself to splitting it between dancers of different types: In fact, for years it was performed that way." Leah quickly sought Katrina's eyes and they exchanged triumphant smiles. Leah knew Katrina had been the best of her group, just as Leah was the best of hers. Leah sat forward in her seat eager to hear the rest of Madame's announcement. It could be only good news now!

Madame cleared her throat and continued. "But I am afraid the stipulations of the Adams grant are quite clear on this particular point. Only one girl can win the scholarship per year. It was a hard decision, but the judges and I finally agreed that the best performance today was given by Katrina Gray."

A cheer went up from the row of contestants. Linda pushed Katrina out into the aisle and she ran up to the stage, where Madame welcomed her with outstretched arms. Leah sat silent, not sure she had heard right.

"They gave it to her only because they pity her!" Pam snarled, and scrambled to her feet. "You danced better!" She looked down at Leah. "You did. Of course if it had been a regular audition with solos and the like!" Pam gave a haughty shrug and headed for the opposite direction of the girls who had gathered around Katrina. Katrina stood in the midst of her friends holding a certificate in one hand, her whole face glowing.

Leah looked after Pam and shook her head sadly. No, she wasn't like Pam at all. She stood up and walked down the row of empty seats toward Katrina. She stepped into the aisle and the crowd parted to let her through.

Katrina's arms wrapped around Leah's neck. "I wish you had won, too! I still want to ask Madame if she'll change her mind."

"No, Katrina, it's in the rules. That's what she said." Leah wasn't sure how, but the next words came out and her voice didn't sound strained at all. "I'm glad you won. You deserved it," Leah said. She couldn't make herself hug Katrina back exuberantly, but Katrina didn't have time to notice. The crowd had closed around her again, and

they herded her toward the lobby and Raul's waiting van.

Somehow Leah ended up in the back of the
van. She kept her eyes focused out the back window and stared at the storefronts and row houses
that blurred by.

When the van pulled into the Academy parking
lot, it seemed as if half the school was waiting.
Leah spotted Kay's red sweater, Alex's black
turtleneck, and Finola's brightly patterned mini-
dress. Leah slipped quietly out the back door of
the van and skirted the crowd as they pressed
forward to see the winner. She ducked into the
school by the side entrance, and even from there
she heard the screams of congratulations.

The cheers grew louder as the crowd neared
the building. The office door was open, and Leah
hid herself behind it. The boys marched in, carry-
ing Katrina high in the air. Everyone was singing
"For She's a Jolly Great Dancer!" Katrina's smile
was perfectly radiant.

Chapter 11

After Kay disappeared down the back stairs and the happy voices of the other kids heading for the party in the cafeteria died down, Leah retraced her steps to the auditorium. A sign dangled from the doorknob: KEEP OUT, it said in bold black print. Leah was relieved: That had to mean no one else would be inside, and what Leah needed now was to be alone. Another, smaller sign, taped to the surface of the door, warned WET PAINT. One of the double doors was open just wide enough for Leah to squeeze in. Paint fumes burned Leah's nostrils. The room was silent. It was after five o'clock and the workmen had already left for the day.

Leah picked up her feet and carefully made her way over the spattered canvas drop cloths. Curious, she noted how pretty the drop cloths were: splattered with pink and yellow and green blobs of paint. All the chairs had been stacked in their rollable metal racks, and with the middle of the room empty, the relatively small auditorium looked grand and huge. Half the proscenium arch was painted a fresh brilliant white, and the other half was still the dirty pale pink that had made more than one generation of SFBA students dub the school auditorium "Rosy Posy Hall." The wood wainscoting had been refinished and polished until it gleamed. Leah absorbed herself with the details of the room as long as she could. It kept her from feeling anything. She wandered to the steps leading up to the stage and sat down, a drop cloth billowing slightly under her. Leah looked away from the stage back out across the empty room. The painters were nearly finished and the whole place was bright and sparkling. Katrina's *Swan Lake* would shine like a jewel in this newly decorated setting.

Leah propped her chin in her hands and stared at the white walls until her tears began. She had made it through the congratulations part okay. She had said all the right things and managed to smile. The smiling part wasn't that hard: After all, Katrina's victory meant more than dancing the lead in *Swan Lake*; it meant she would get to stay at SFBA. Leah was happy for her. But she sensed Katrina knew her well enough to understand why Leah wouldn't show up at her party.

Leah drew her legs up to her chest. She felt very small in the huge, empty room. She felt dumb, and humiliated—not because of Katrina winning but because of herself. How could she have believed that she was someone special? As if she had been born with a pair of golden toe shoes on her feet, with a brilliant future as an internationally acclaimed ballerina as her birthright. She couldn't even get the lead in SFBA's first full-length ballet of the year! And it wasn't as if she hadn't been warned about something just like this happening sooner or later: Diana Chang had

told her several times over the past few months
that other girls were as talented as Leah, if not
more. Diana hadn't quite spelled it out, but Leah
knew the older dancer felt Leah's abilities were
highly overrated. Leah had chalked up Diana's
remarks to a rivalry that persisted between them
in spite of outwardly friendly behavior to each
other.

Only a few weeks ago Andrei would have chosen
Pam over Leah to dance in his newly choreo-
graphed ballet for the fund-raising gala, except
that Pam managed to get hurt. Leah had won the
coveted role only by default. And now there was
Finola. It hurt to admit it, but no one at SFBA,
including Alex, could hold a candle to the English
girl. With Finola at the same barre, holding the
Golden Gate Award as Leah did meant very little
in the long run at all.

But Leah hadn't wanted to see the writing on
the wall. The truth was that she was not the best
student at SFBA. She was good, and talented, and
all the other things Madame and her old teacher
Hannah Greene had claimed she was. But good
and talented weren't enough anymore. The world
of ballet was a competitive place, and over the
past few months Leah had come to realize that to
even have a chance to get to the top in the world
of dance she had to begin by being the best
student at the San Francisco Ballet Academy. But
she wasn't. If she were the best, winning the
Louise Adams Scholarship would have been easy.

Leah suddenly seemed to see her future: drafty
school auditoriums, small regional ballet companies, skimpy, ill-fitting tutus, and occasional fill-in
jobs in the corps of a second-rate company in a
small city. Suddenly she wondered if she wanted

any kind of future as a dancer. Leah began to sob loudly and for the second time in two days she cried in a way she hadn't in years. She slipped down a little on the stairs and rested her damp face on her arms, her shoulders heaving as she wept her heart out.

"Leah?"

Andrei's voice made Leah jump. She sat up. He looked a little embarrassed as he stood at the foot of the short flight of steps that led from the auditorium floor to the stage. He was holding a large package wrapped clumsily in brown paper and heavy twine. Keeping her eyes on the package, Leah self-consciously rubbed the tears and the mascara off her cheeks. She didn't have any tissues with her, so she used the sleeve of her pale pink sweater.

Andrei didn't say anything else right away, and Leah appreciated that. It gave her time to pull herself together. She pushed her hair back from her face and stood up. In her wool skirt, knee socks, and cardigan she felt like an awkward high school girl in front of the famous Russian dancer. She kept her eyes lowered until she was sure she had mastered her feelings. When she looked up she noticed a dab of white paint on one leg of Andrei's new suede pants. It made him seem more human and reminded Leah he wasn't just a famous dancer but also a good friend.

Finally Andrei spoke. "I heard the news. So Katrina can stay in the school now. That is good."

"Yes," Leah said with great effort. "It's very good. I'm glad about that." She looked up sharply and said, "I mean that. I would have felt terrible about her having to leave next semester."

"As terrible as your not being able to dance the Odette/Odile role?"

"What do you think?" Leah countered. Then her shoulders sagged and she rubbed her fist across her forehead. Like her mother, Leah always got headaches the minute she started crying. "I'm sorry, Andrei. I didn't mean to snap at you." Leah settled her dance bag on her shoulder and started to leave the room.

"I would feel terrible, too," Andrei admitted.

Leah spun around on her heel. "Andrei Levintoff, what would you know about not winning competitions?" she said, exasperated.

Andrei surprised her with a low laugh. "I know much about not winning competitions. I have won only a few. No more after I was fourteen and went to the advanced classes in my school." He motioned toward the stairs and started to sit down.

Leah wasn't sure she believed Andrei, but he was trying his best to make her feel better, and somehow it was working. Leah stared at the cloth-draped step and after a moment's hesitation settled down next to him.

For a moment they sat next to each other, listening to the companionable sound of the rain on the skylight. "Losing this competition is the worst thing that's happened to me here so far," Leah said gently.

Andrei nodded and swept his long hair out of his eyes.

Leah chose her next words carefully before going on. "I know this sounds awful, but I never pictured myself losing. Not just to Katrina, but to anyone really—" Thinking of Alex and Finola, she added quickly, "Anyone who was competing today, anyway." Leah intently regarded her hands.

"I guess that sounds pretty stuck-up, doesn't it?" she asked in a small voice.

"Not at all, Leah. It is what you have to think if you want to be a great dancer. I think that way, too. I do not get every role I want. Until now, of course." Andrei made a face. "Because I am famous for leaving my country, people will give me anything. It is only because a new Russian danseur in the West is like a circus act and everyone wants to see me. So now whatever I want, I get. But you have to think you are the best or the judges will never believe it."

Leah couldn't hold back her feelings anymore. "But I wonder if it's worth it!" she cried. "I mean, if you're not good enough to actually be the best, and you only think you are, then why do it?"

"Because you are born to dance, and that's all that matters," Andrei answered. "You are a wonderful dancer, Leah. But today Katrina danced with more heart than you. She has a different quality and that is why the judges picked her. You know, she has become a much better dancer even since I come here."

"I know that." Leah didn't trust herself to say more. The fact that Katrina won was all right with Leah. The problem was that both of them couldn't win.

"Too bad," he said, seeming to read Leah's mind, "one of you could not dance the Black Swan and one the White! But there was only one scholarship, no?"

"Yes," Leah said.

Andrei put his hand on Leah's shoulder then tousled her hair. It was still damp from the rain, but his touch warmed her, and she managed a weak smile.

"You see, Leah, you cannot be greedy. You have the Golden Gate Award, and that is quite an honor. You cannot win all the money and get every lead role in every performance." Andrei got up and dusted off his pants. "I think," he said matter-of-factly, "maybe the judges think that, too."

Leah gave him a blank look, letting his comment sink in. There was a chance that the judges didn't pass over Leah because she wasn't good enough. Maybe they just wanted to distribute the roles. Maybe she would get the next one.

"By the way, I thought you would like this." Andrei awkwardly shoved the large package toward her. "Perhaps I should have brought it to the boardinghouse, but I was afraid that Alex might get the wrong idea—I make no present yet for her!"

Leah took the package from Andrei and ran her fingers around the edge. She loved trying to guess what might be inside a present, to put off the moment of opening it. Leah's fingers paused on the corner and slipped under a bit of twine. The package did have a familiar feel to it. "Oh, Andrei," Leah cried, "the painting, the painting of me!" She gaped at Andrei, wide-eyed. "I can have it?" He just grinned and Leah began to tear at the wrapping. "This is a wonderful painting," she said, holding it at arm's length and studying the abstract swirls of pink and golden paint. It didn't really look like Leah, or like a person, really, but it expressed movement and dance and joy. "It's Juliet, it really is," Leah said, awed. She turned to Andrei, a soft glow in her eyes.

"You like it? Let me wrap it again. It is too wet outside." As he fumbled with the twine, he said, "I thought if you like we could go to the Opera

House together now and you could watch my *Corsaire* from the audience. I can put the canvas in my car and—"

Leah shook her head. Andrei's present and their talk had made her feel better, but she still wanted to be alone. "Thanks, but not tonight, Andrei. It's been, well, a rather long day!" She smiled timidly. "Thanks for everything."

Andrei carried the painting to the hall for her and Leah waved good-bye as he went out the front door. She headed in the direction of the basement and the lockers. She could stop in Raul's office on the way and see if he'd give her a ride home in the van. If not, she could leave the painting at school until tomorrow.

"There she is!" Katrina's voice exclaimed from the far end of a row of metal lockers that stretched the length of the hall outside the cafeteria.

Leah stopped in her tracks. Next to Katrina were Alex and Finola, and Kay's curly head was just visible behind them. Leah felt very embarrassed. She had congratulated Katrina back at the theater, and Alex had held her hand through thick and thin the last couple of days, but she hadn't said a word to Kay since their argument. And Finola—the thought of her last encounter with the English girl turned Leah's whole face red.

"You missed the party!" Alex cried, hurrying toward her. Her dark eyes took in the large package Leah was holding under one arm. Alex arched her eybrows in a question, but before Leah could tell her about the painting, the other girls crowded around.

"You're not going to believe what happened!" Kay blurted out, then seemed to remember that she and Leah weren't supposed to be talking. She blushed and looked down.

"Listen, Kay—" Leah started to apologize.

But Kay didn't give her a chance. "Oh, Leah! I was such a jerk. I should never have said the things I did to you. It was wrong and unfair and—" She paused to take a breath. "And not just to you." Kay turned around and looked right into Katrina's startled eyes. "To you, too, Katrina. And I'm not just saying this because you won. I think it was wrong of me—of all of us—to underestimate you."

"You can say that again," Finola asserted with a wry little smile.

"Well, you always knew I could do it," Katrina said to Finola after a moment's awkward silence. Then she startled everyone by throwing her arm around Leah. "And so did you, Leah. You told me right from the beginning that I had as good a chance as anyone else here. If you hadn't said that, I wouldn't have had the nerve to compete."

Leah felt she didn't deserve that, but no one gave her a chance to protest.

"If you ask me, Leah gave Katrina the biggest compliment of all!" Finola said, smiling directly at Leah. "She was really scared Katrina would win!"

Leah's mouth dropped open in surprise. Then she started laughing. "Thank goodness this isn't a drama school! I'd fail out after two days. And I thought I was putting on such a good act and not seeming jealous or anything." Speaking of her jealousy and fear openly with her friends made all Leah's bad feelings disappear. Of course, the girls would be constantly in competition with one another over the next few years. But Alex had always maintained they could, if they really tried, stay friends through it all, and Leah believed her.

"Well, when you hear the next bit of good news you're not going to have to act at all," Alex said with great confidence. She flung her long black braid over her shoulder and waited for everyone else to be quiet. She cleared her throat dramatically. "Because you skipped the party just now, you are the last to know."

"Know what?" Leah urged. She hated when Alex kept her in suspense.

"Diana was in the cafeteria, and she just happened to mention that you, Leah Kimberly Stephenson, will be dancing in the Adams evening ballet after all."

Leah's face fell slightly. Of course she'd be dancing in the corps. All of the girls would.

But Kay obviously couldn't stand keeping Leah in suspense any longer. She leaned closer to Leah and announced, "You're going to have a really big solo!"

"Me?" Leah asked, startled. Quickly she reviewed the ballet in her head trying to remember the solos, but she drew a blank. "In what act?"

"The first!" the other girls all exclaimed at once.

Leah was still puzzled. The first act was the prince's twenty-first birthday party. It featured peasant and courtly corps dancing. What solos were in it for her? "A solo?" she asked again.

"Well, it's not exactly a solo, Kay," Finola answered. She propped herself against the wall and stretched out her long legs. "You'll be dancing with none other than—" She sounded a flourish in her high soprano voice and then motioned for the other girls to help her break the news.

"With Pamela Hunter!" they announced in unison.

Leah shook her head slowly in disbelief. "Pam and I are dancing together?"

"Uh-huh!" Kay nodded. She rubbed her hands in gleeful anticipation. She obviously knew that Leah and Pam working on the same stage was going to make for a lot of good SFBA gossip.

"It's the pas de trois in the first act," Alex explained. "You, Pam, and probably Kenny Rotolo."

Leah let out a small, dismal moan. "I don't believe this. Of all the rotten luck. Why couldn't I just be a plain old swan, in the back row, anonymous?"

"Because you're too good. And you'll be the first ballerina the audience will see, Leah," Katrina said, putting her arm around Leah's shoulder. "So you didn't lose at all!"

"No, I didn't, Katrina. I didn't lose you—and that's what matters the most," Leah said from the bottom of her heart. "You're a great dancer, and a great friend." She turned to everyone else. "You all are!"

GLOSSARY

Adagio—Slow tempo dance steps; essential to sustaining controlled body line. When dancing with a partner, the term refers to support of ballerina.

Allegro—Quick, lively dance step.

Arabesque—Dancer stands on one leg and extends the other leg straight back while holding the arms in graceful positions.

> *Arabesque penchée*—The dancer's whole body leans forward over the supporting leg. (Also referred to as penché.)

Assemblé—A jump in which the two feet are brought together in the air before the dancer lands on the ground in fifth position.

Attitude turns—The *attitude* is a classical position in which the working or raised leg is bent at the knee and extended to the back, as if wrapped around the dancer. An *attitude turn* is a turn performed in this position.

Ballon—Illusion of suspending in air.

Barre—The wooden bar along the wall of every ballet studio. Work at the barre makes up the first part of practice.

Battement—Throwing the leg as high as possible into the air to the front, the side, and the back. Several variations.

  Battement en cloche—Swinging the leg as high as possible to the back and to the front to loosen the hip joint.

Bourrée—Small, quick steps usually done on toes. Many variations.

Brisé—A jump off one foot in which the legs are beaten together in the air.

Centre work—The main part of practice; performing steps on the floor after barre work.

Chainé—A series of short, usually fast turns on pointe by which a dancer moves across the stage.

Corps de ballet—Any and all members of the ballet who are not soloists.

Dégagé—Extension with toe pointed in preparation for a ballet step.

Developpé—The slow raising and unfolding of one leg until it is high in the air (usually done in pas de deux, or with support of barre or partner).

Echappé—A movement in which the dancer springs up from fifth position onto pointe in second position. Also a jump.

Fouetté—A step in which the dancer is on one leg and uses the other leg in a sort of whipping movement to help the body turn.

Jeté—A jump from one foot onto the other in which working leg appears to be thrown in the air.

Mazurka—A Polish national dance.

Pas de deux—Dance for 2 dancers. ("Pas de trois" means dance for 3 dancers, and so on.)

Pas de chat—Meaning "step of the cat." A light, springing movement. The dancer jumps and draws one foot up to the knee of the opposite leg, then draws up the other leg, one after the other, traveling diagonally across the stage.

Penché—Referring to an arabesque penchée.

Piqué—Direct step onto pointe without bending the knee of the working leg.

Plié—With feet and legs turned out, a movement by which the dancer bends both knees outward over her toes, leaving her heels on the ground.

　Demi plié—Bending the knees as far as possible leaving the heels on the floor.

　Grand plié—Bending knees all the way down

letting the heels come off the floor (except in second position).

Pointe work—Exercises performed in pointe (toe) shoes.

Port de bras—Position of the dancer's arms.

Posé—Stepping onto pointe with a straight leg.

Positions—There are five basic positions of the feet and arms that all ballet dancers must learn.

Rétiré—Drawing the toe of one foot to the opposite knee.

Rond de jambe à terre—An exercise performed at the barre to loosen the hip joint: performed first outward (*en dehors*) and then inward (*en dedans*). The working leg is extended first to the front with the foot fully pointed and then swept around to the side and back and through first position to the front again. The movement is then reversed, starting from the fourth position back and sweeping around to the side and front. (The foot traces the shape of the letter "D" on the floor.)

Sissonne—With a slight plié, dancer springs into the air from the fifth position, and lands on one foot with a demi plié with the other leg extended to the back, front, or side. The foot of the extended leg is then closed to the supporting foot.

Tendu—Stretching or holding a certain position or movement.

Tour en l'air—A spectacular jump in which the dancer leaps directly upwards and turns one, two, or three times before landing.

Here's a look at what's ahead in CURTAIN CALL, the sixth book in Fawcett's "Satin Slippers" series for GIRLS ONLY

Leah felt as if she were going to explode, and she was definitely not in the mood to deal with Pam. Leah had managed not to talk to her all day so far, and she was about to tell Pam to get lost when Pam stopped her battements at the barre and dropped down onto the floor at Leah's side. "Leah, I don't blame you one bit. Why, I wouldn't speak to me either. Not at all."

"Don't flatter yourself, Pam," Kenny said brusquely. He was lying on the floor in a shoulder stand, stretching out his back and legs. He held them straight up for a moment, then eased them down with his toes brushing the floor behind his head. "Leah's angry at Robson, not you." Leah took a deep breath. She scrambled to her feet and walked away from Kenny and Pam. Putting one hand on the barre, she began to do her warm-up pliés all over again.

Pam stood up, too. She put her opposite hand on the barre and faced Leah. "I know you saw me last night. I was listening to your conversation with your friend. I shouldn't have done that. I'm sorry."

Leah was halfway down in a grand plié when Pam said that. She straightened up quickly and shoved the sleeves of her blue cardigan up on her arms. "Did I hear that right? Did you just admit that you were eavesdropping on my conversation?"

Pam looked down at the floor and studied her feet.

"Yes." She looked up and her green eyes were wide and innocent-looking. "I apologize. I shouldn't have done that."

"Listen, Pam," Leah began, for the life of her unable to fathom what was going on in Pam's head, "if you shouldn't have done it, why did you?"

"I—I couldn't help myself." Pam tugged down the back of her leotard and began practicing a series of battements tendu. The sharp, strong movement of her foot as she pointed it out first in front of her, then to the side and to the back, contrasted harshly with her shy, humble expression.

"Pamela Hunter, I don't believe you."

"But it's true—I couldn't." Pam looked quickly at Kenny, then lowered her voice so only Leah could hear. "Don't you understand?" she said, and placed an urgent hand on Leah's arm. "I know it's awful, but as long as I can remember people haven't liked me very much. My mother says they're jealous. I guess I'm a strong dancer and I'm attractive—"

Leah's blue eyes narrowed as she tried to figure out Pam. On the one hand, Pam was admitting she'd done wrong, but on the other, she was trying to excuse her behavior on the grounds that people were jealous of her good looks and talent. A warning bell went off in Leah's head, but she wanted to hear Pam out. The redhead's admission of guilt had taken Leah offguard, but perhaps this was Pam's way of trying to be friends.

"I know how stuck-up that all sounds, but you know how people are sometimes. They get jealous about the darnedest things. Anyway, I got this nasty habit, and it's so hard to shake. I can't help but want to listen to see if people are talking about me and—" Pam broke off and bit her lip, and Leah detected the glint of tears in Pam's cool green eyes.

"So you listened to me to see if I was going to talk about you to my best friend back home," Leah finished for her in a quiet, flat voice. She took a deep breath and found herself smiling—it was a small smile, but it was enough to reassure Pam. Pam nodded and smiled back, too.

Leah cleared her throat. "Pam, if you want people to be your friends, you have to trust them. I might have said something to Chrissy about you last night. Would hearing me say it—whether it was bad or good—make you really feel any better about me or about yourself?"

Slowly Pam shook her head back and forth. For the second time in two days she reminded Leah of a little girl. "I hadn't thought of it that way. I just wanted to know what people were saying about me so I'd know how to defend myself."

"But if you didn't do things like eavesdrop," Leah said sharply, "you wouldn't have to defend yourself in the first place."

"Oh, Leah." Pam folded her hands in a pretty pleading gesture—the same one she had used with Madame the day before. "I never thought of it like that. I promise, I'll never ever eavesdrop on you—" Pam covered her mouth and let out a cute, convincing giggle. "I mean, on *anyone* again!"

"Places!" Christopher roared. Pam and Leah both jumped a little at the sound of his voice. Leah yanked off her leg warmers and started to her spot behind the strip of masking tape that marked the wings.

"Psssst!"

Leah turned around ever so slightly and cast a questioning glance in Pam's direction.

"Friends?" Pam asked in a stage whisper.

Kenny whipped around and glared at her. He made a sound of disgust and shook his head.

Leah ignored Kenny and whispered back to Pam, "Friends."

ABOUT THE AUTHOR

Elizabeth Bernard has had a lifelong passion for dance. Her interest and background in ballet is wide and various and has led to many friendships and acquaintances in the ballet and dance world. Through these connections she has had the opportunity to witness firsthand a behind-the-scenes world of dance seldom seen by non-dancers. She is familiar with the stuff of ballet life: the artistry, the dedication, the fierce competition, the heartaches, the pains, and disappointments. She is the author of over a dozen books for young adults, including titles in the bestselling COUPLES series, published by Scholastic, and the SISTERS series, published by Fawcett.